Big Magical Dreams

Chesca

and the

Spirit of Grace

by Lara O'Brien

Lara.

CHESCA AND THE SPIRIT OF GRACE

ISBN: 978-0-9896752-0-8

Map of Howth region of Ireland copyright © 2010 by Sorcha O'Farrell. Used by permission.

Illuminated typeface is Goudy Initialen by Dieter Steffmann

Cover design by Chris Beatrice

Dedicated to my family, rare and special creatures,

~ BIG magical Love ~

And to Howth Riding Stables,

for the sweet memories,

and all the horses that we loved there.

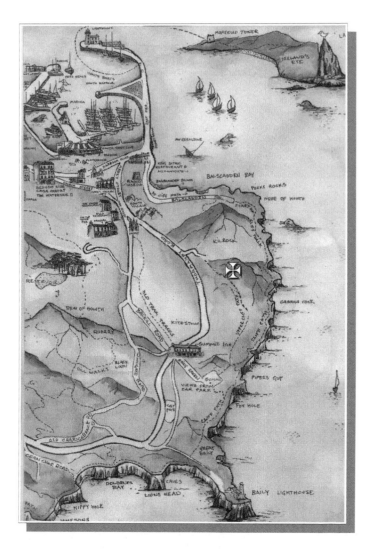

Map of Howth

The East Mountain and the Brandy Banks

Chapter 1

"If Malley said jump up on my back and we'll go for a wild gallop down the Boreen, I'd do it in a heart beat," Chesca said, and nodded at Mouse. A cute fat mouse sat propped on the comforter of her bed. Outside, the wind blew in gusts and rattled the old farmhouse windows.

"But," said the Mouse.

"But," Chesca threw her hands in the air, "Da continues to say no! No, not yet. No, it's not the right time. NO."

Mouse trembled. "He's dead right, your Da."

Chesca pulled on her brown dusty boots. "I believe in today, Mouse, and Malley does too."

"Would you not be afraid, Chesca? He's a bit of a temper on him."

"He's a gent of a horse."

"He's the biggest horse I've ever seen. I'd never want to cross him."

"And you never will, silly. He's a protector of all things Howth. Howth is forever. Howth is magic. Howth rules, and we are Howth. You're a Howth mouse and I'm a Howth girl."

"There is that," Mouse said and jumped into Chesca's denim pocket and rolled into a ball, not to be seen. Chesca grabbed a small book, *A Magical Horse Show*, from the nook by the window and shoved it under her pillow to read again tonight. She tightened her chaps, bolted out the door, and slid backwards down the banister, minding not to squeeze Mouse, then landed lightly on her feet.

It was dawn and Chesca's parents were already in the kitchen. Her father grabbed a piece of toast from the toaster and knocked back a glass of OJ. Her mother put a pan of scrambled eggs on the table.

"When can I ride Malley?" Chesca said.

Her father laughed and nearly choked on his toast, coughing, shaking his head, for she asked every morning without fail, and her asking had become a bit of a joke for him.

"I'm serious Da. What's your problem?"

"Claire dear, will you talk sense to her? I've cows to milk," he said and winked at Ma. Her Da was always busy with the cows and left the horses to Ma. He tossed her hair with his large chapped hands and strode out the door for a day of working in the dairy.

The O'Brien farm sat on the side of a mountain and in the dawn light she could see the outline of her favorite field: the Brandy Banks. In the old days, smugglers used to bootleg alcohol from the cove under the field. Chesca loved history and knew all the historic and wondrous events that had taken place on the mountain. Well…she thought she did.

Malley, the best stallion to walk Ireland, was out there roaming the moors, keeping an eye on things, making sure all the animals were fine. One time, a horse thief crossed him and ended up in hospital for three long weeks. Malley had said he was an *amadan*—Irish for not too smart.

"I'd better hurry," Chesca said.

"Why?"

"Malley's dying to tell me a story about a girl just like me, who had a golden stallion and *wasn't* allowed to ride him either."

Ma turned away from the mirror that hung over the mantel. She pulled her hair into a bun and tied a green scarf at the nape of her neck. Her own dark hair and green eyes made people stop in the street and say Chesca was the 'spit of her.'

"I know it sounds funny, but Malley has the art of telling serious stories in a fun way. He's such a good storyteller." Chesca said. "Did you ever hear about the man who came to steal the chickens and ended up hanging from the cliff ledge?"

"Holy God," Ma said. "Tell me that didn't happen?

"It did. And he'd a bunch of gorse stuck down his trousers!"

"Who did that to him?"

"Malley and Turkey, of course."

The way Ma looked at her, Chesca thought she would do the prayer to St Jude she did sometimes, the prayer for lost things and causes.

But she didn't. She said, "Listen, I think he's not the only storyteller. Ches, why don't you talk less to the animals and more to the kids at the stables at Bailey Farm, or from school, or church? Aunt Dena said you need more time in the clubs with other kids your age. How about summer camp at the castle?"

"What would she know about kids or camps? Seriously, Ma? Only really weird kids go to those camps, and I'm not weird. I don't care what they say." She swung the fridge door open and grabbed a piece of cheese.

Her mother took her by the shoulders and turned her around to face her. "It's time you opened up to the idea of having friends. If you keep acting like you don't care, you'll never make one. Not a single girl your age will want to know you if you keep sending such hostile signals. I saw the sign on the gate you know?

Chesca shrugged, feigning innocence.

"*Keep off our Mountain MM.* I know you wrote it." Ma shook her finger. "It's not good for business either. You know, Ches, everyone needs a friend, even you."

"I have more friends than I can count and they all have four legs and a tail. The very best kind." She looked outside. The wind blew and a sparrow flew out from under the barn roof. Her mother just didn't understand.

Chesca had been listening and hearing the animals since she was seven years old, the day that MM—Mary Murphy, the show-jumping champion from the next farm over, called her a wuss for crying, sobbing, when quirky ol' Pig Senior died. Mary Murphy told her to grow up, that eventually everything dies. It was the day a black cloud come round her.

She swore never to think of death again, as if by not thinking about it, or talking about, especially with MM;

maybe the dark and empty feeling would stay away, bypass her, and skip the farm completely.

She swore never to speak to MM again. A promise she had kept.

Instead, she wished to love with all her heart what she knew to be true and loyal, her family and her animals. Nothing else mattered.

Later that same day as she sat on a bale of hay in the barn, sniffing, lamenting Pig Senior, Malley, the O'Brien's champion of stallions, and leader of horses for miles around, took a few steps toward her and stood so near she could touch him, and she did. She put her hand out and touched his silky nose, something she had never done before. The light fell on the threads of gold that ran through his chestnut coat. She remembered how her heart beat like a drum and the warmth of his breath and the glimpse of a spark in his eye, and she did not feel afraid by his size or his mighty energy. She felt a soft breeze embrace her even though it was December. She thought she heard the word calm. She continued staring deep into his eyes, knowing something had changed, shifted, something magical was happening.

Then it happened. Polly, her black and white dog, laid her head on Chesca's knee and whimpered, "I'll miss Pig Senior, too."

Chesca said calmly, as if it was a very normal thing to hear your dog talking to you.

"I know you will, Polly," and they put their heads together and cried some more.

That was the very first time Chesca heard any animal talk.

They might neigh, or grunt or bark or bleat, but she understood every word.

Chesca looked at her Ma clearing the dishes away and whispered. "You don't hear what I hear, Ma."

A soft voice floated on the wind...*Chesca...*

"Got to run," Chesca sang. She was about to cartwheel out the kitchen door into the hall, because that's what she does. She cartwheels, handstands, hand-walks and somersaults when possible, but instead she turned.

Her mother leaned over the sink, massaging her head.

"Wait. Who are you meeting?" Chesca said.

"Oh, Mr. Davis from the bank."

"That baldie ol' ba…"

"Chesca. Language!"

"I *was* going to say, banker," Chesca shook her head slowly, as if her mother was the child. "What's he want, anyway?"

"Something about loans, insurance, money," she said with a sigh. "They all want money, money, money. It makes my head hurt."

"It'll be fine. Da fixes everything."

Polly started barking at the front door.

"Well, yes, he will," Ma said. "But don't forget, we need to talk later, about those camps."

"Polly's calling me," and Chesca was out the door.

A soft breeze greeted her. There was the faint sound of laughter coming from the lane, then a whisper.

Come along, Chesca, stories to be told, very important...

She ran as fast as she could out of the yard. Whispering Lane was calling.

Chapter 2

he clouds parted and the early morning light shone through the oaks and evergreens as Chesca ran past the farm gate into Whispering Lane. The smell of lush grass and sea spray drifted in the air. Something else was alive in the air. It was magic. Howth is Magic—it even said it on the tourist brochure in the chamber of commerce.

"Why can't everyone see that?" Chesca said.

What? Whispered Lane.

"Howth is Magic."

Magic is everywhere, in everyone...

"You're very deep, Lane. Very wise."

I'm just old, whispered Lane and the trees shook and the dewdrops fell on Chesca's head like a shower. She ran a little faster now and Wind blew the hair around her face and whistled past her ears, playing with her. Wind loved to play, unlike Lane who was too old and didn't move much at all.

The brochures tried to get it right but how they expected to capture the beauty of Howth Head in one little pamphlet, Chesca never understood. To see the lower meadows roll out and down to the ocean, the upper fields crowned in wild purple heather and yellow gorse, over three hundred acres of untamed moors to the summit of the mountain, the Bailey lighthouse and Wicklow Mountains. Well, even with a little picture in the corner, it couldn't capture the life of her, the wild and the wondrous. Yes, Howth is Magic.

Wind blew north to play with a drifting sailboat.

She stood overlooking the Brandy Banks, surrounded by old stone walls and steeped in history. An old ruin of a cottage sat beside the beaten track and circle where her animals met. The fields and meadows all fell away to the cliffs and down to the beach, cove, village and harbor. The Irish Sea inhaled and exhaled, wave following wave. Chesca looked at the Mountain and down to the sea.

"She breathes," she said and threw her hands toward the ocean, like a character in a Shakespearean play.

"I see them," squeaked Mouse, peeking out of Chesca's pocket. "The circle is taking shape. Wait now, are they all here?" Mouse's eyes darted to and fro, counting. Chesca tallied each four-legged friend, all the time looking for one in particular.

The animals gathered from every direction. The Kerry cows strolled up from the dairy, chatting away as girls do. By the swing of their hips and the swish of their tails, Chesca knew they were relaxed after the milking, having delivered the finest milk in the whole of Dublin, if not Ireland. Turkey hopped in a circle, then jumped onto the branch of the oak tree. Donkey stood, dreaming, looking at the clouds, and the ponies and horses grazed by the cottage.

Rooster, a highly devoted and flamboyant artist, flapped and jumped around a canvas lying in the buttercups. She had taught him to hold a paintbrush in his beak last year and he painted with an obsession these days. He dipped his brush into his pots of clay mixes of brown, pink and black and captured the Brandy Banks and Babbling Brook on a canvas feed bag, stretched by his adoring hens over a frame made of driftwood.

"Our Rooster could out paint Picasso, any day." Chesca said.

A smoky, sultry voice made them swing around.

"Isn't he fantastic, darlings?"

"Star," Chesca said, delighted, as her bay mare placed her fetlocks forward and stretched her rump in the air, a good pose for toning the back muscles. Star batted her eyelashes and held her head in the coy way of a starlet.

"Ready for the meeting, sweeties?" Star said, doing one last stretch.

"I don't see Malley," said Chesca.

"Who knows where he is," said Star, throwing her head back dramatically, because...well because she was a drama queen. "Out fighting for justice no doubt, but he'll be here, nothing could stop him."

Chesca vaulted on to her back. Star was not only a dramatic queen but a super dancer and did three quick side steps then shot forward, galloping down the slope with her bay coat gleaming in the sunlight. At the circle she skidded to a halt and Chesca went flying in the air, somersaulted and landed on her feet, right in the center.

Chesca's acrobatics had earned her a reputation. She was always trick riding, vaulting, galloping sideways, and backwards. Forever making up new rides with music in her head, she could spend hours daydreaming of scenes, and characters and lights and applause. When she could, she practiced her trick riding for hours on end.

She knew she had many reputations around the village and being incapable of sitting still was the least of it. Some people were not very nice. Audrey Clemens, the girl who sat next to her in class, called her mad because she saw Chesca talking to a mouse. Audrey Clemens was a gossip, just like her mother, and told everyone in school that Chesca was crazy. Chesca told her to go and...

"Nice landing," Rooster cock-a-doodled and let the whole of the mountain know she had arrived and the meeting was in order.

"Morning boys," said Chesca, and gave them both a hug. Turkey went puce. Only Chesca noticed; it's hard to see a Turkey blush. She made a little curtsey to the Kerry cows.

Pig came galloping out from behind the hawthorn tree with Polly chasing after. "I heard there was suspicious movement near the summit last night," Pig grunted with excitement. They all stopped suddenly as a pounding beat cut through the air, followed by a piercing whinny.

Mouse screeched, covering her ears with her paws. All eyes went to the top of the East Mountain. Chesca's heart beat faster as each hoof hit the ground not taking her eyes off the heather.

"Move," barked Polly, and the animals stood back.

The golden-chestnut stallion soared over heather and fern, jumping stone walls. He looked wild, like one of those mountain Mustangs, but bigger and stronger and fiercer. His tail streamed out behind him, his long mane flowed down his neck, and his thick forelock covered his eyes. Mouse was right, Chesca thought, you wouldn't want to cross him, but that's what made him so mighty. He looked a lot scarier than he was, unless you were asking for it—then you were a goner.

The Kerry Cows formed a line as Malley thundered down the mountain. Grass divots flew as he skidded to a halt. Chesca stood her ground. Malley's nostrils were fire-red as he took a huge breath and looked at his friends. Softening his gaze, he took two small steps, his massive hooves cutting into the soft dewy soil. Ever so gently, he nickered.

"It's good to see you in the first light, Chesca."

"Malley," she nodded, but got stuck for words. His presence seemed to pull her up, higher, make her feel like she was more than she was. "I hear there was action at the summit last night?" she said.

"Some old man got lost, he was wobbling and singing and heading straight for the cliff. I had to frighten him to his senses and away from the edge."

She watched him as he accounted for each four-legged friend, his eyes roaming the circle. He looked up into the tree to check on Turkey, who was now settling down, and he counted each hen and each cow. He took a deep breath. "It's time," he said, with a nod to her. "You wanted to know about Grace and the history of Howth, Chesca? And I want to tell you a story that is important to us all."

Chapter 3

hesca sat cross-legged in the circle surrounded by her friends and settled in for the story. A huge hawthorn tree towered over the cottage like an umbrella.

"Once upon a time," Malley began, taking a deep breath, "there was a girl born a chieftain on the west coast of Ireland. Her name was Grace O'Malley. When she was a young girl, her father refused to let her ride the family's warrior horse, a strong fierce stallion that fought in every leading battle. He refused to let her sail with him, insisting she stay at home with her mother and study her lessons and prepare to marry. She didn't want to stay home, she wanted wild and exciting adventure. To prove herself to her father, she cut off her hair to look like a boy and stole away on his ship to trade in foreign lands. Later, when she was a young woman with a ship of her own, she sailed into Howth Harbor and docked right there...on the West Pier." He swung his nose in the direction of the harbor and the village. "Not only was she a chieftain, she was a pirate queen."

"Pirate queen!" Chesca said, bolting upright. "Why did she come here?"

"Yes, why?" said Star.

"She came for dinner," said Malley.

"Dinner?" they all said.

"Tired from her travels, she stopped for dinner with the Earl of Howth at Howth Castle. But, on her arrival at the castle, a servant turned her away, telling her the Earl was busy and would not see her."

The animals looked at each other. The softest breeze rippled across the heather on the banks behind them.

"By refusing her his hospitality, the Earl had insulted her greatly. Grace was furious. She spurred her horse from the castle doors so fast that she nearly knocked over a small boy playing with a stick and ball by the iron gates. Pulling suddenly on the reins, she had an idea. Grace took the young boy on an adventure back to her castle in the West to the absolute fury of the Earl, for she had taken his grandson."

"That's kidnapping," Polly said.

"Fair play to her," Chesca said. "Those Earls are a shower of…"

"I'm sure Grace only borrowed him," Pig grunted impatiently, wanting Malley to continue.

"The Earl followed after her in his ship, like that," Malley nodded at the *Asgard*, sailing out past the little Island of Ireland's Eye.

"Did they battle?" asked Mouse, her brow beginning to crease.

"As he landed on the shores of Clew Bay," Malley continued, "a lone figure stood waiting for him. Grace, tall and slender, but tough—she was the leader of a large part of Ireland."

"What did she wear?" asked Star. "Was she glamorous?"

"She was. Dressed in her finest velvet green cloak, heavy with rubies and diamonds. Her chestnut hair held back in a gold clasp with pearls. Behind her, on the meadow above the shore, was the boy, on a young golden horse.

"'I have only one request to ensure your boy's safe return,' Grace called out. 'I ask that you keep a place set for a tired traveler and that your gates be always kept open.'"

Malley looked down past the town to the manicured gardens and the tip of the tower of Howth Castle.

"And...?" asked Chesca.

"Grace had become quite fond of the boy, and she gave him a parting gift—the chestnut stallion, a colt from her own mare. The Earl agreed to her request and they sailed back to Howth with the stallion. The boy would keep this horse and ride him over the castle grounds until he died, which was not too long after."

"And on a blustery day the stallion broke away from the castle, uneasy without the boy, and galloped to a farm on the east side of the mountain, where he found a home with the O'Brien clan. And his bloodline has remained here to this day."

"Wait...you're...you're Malley as in *Grace O'Malley*?"

Malley nodded, and he held his head high. Everyone began cheering or stamping their hooves.

"The very same. He would become one of the fiercest champions of the people of Howth. I'm a direct descendant of that stallion."

"Magnificent," Chesca said. "I knew it." She scrambled to her feet and patted him on the neck, clapping him, like he had just won the Kentucky Derby. She hugged him, stood and admired him for a minute, smiled, then held out her hand towards him, like she was presenting him for the first time, and everyone cheered again.

"My Irish king," she nodded, as the guillemots and kittiwakes sang out. "So...was this Grace girl beautiful?"

"In heart and mind," he nickered in a low tone, "and she was a brave, strong, fair pirate, and a very clever woman who loved her land. And above all, she was a survivor."

"You know, I'd love to be a pirate queen," Chesca said, searching the skies imagining herself in robes and jewels and fighting off girls that called her crazy, battling it out with Mary Murphy. "A pirate chieftain, for justice and freedom and love of land."

"Aren't you a queen already?" said Malley.

Chesca hesitated, and held her finger in the air.

"Me too," said Star, throwing her forelock back. "I want to be Grace's magnificent mare. I want to wear that cloak with the fancy brooch. My mother told me, I was born to be a star. She took one look at the star on my head…"

It was true that Star had a white star on her forehead, and she reminded everyone who would listen, that she was born a bright star.

"And," Rooster finished, "someday you would be the star of Dublin." He crowed with laughter, then Donkey brayed, and the hens cackled following his lead.

"You in a cloak," snorted Pig.

Star batted her eyelashes. The indignity. She was not impressed. She would show them. Anyone gifted a star must shine.

Chesca could hear Ma calling them, "*Hup, hup, hup!*" echoing around the mountain, the start of a new workday. Polly began barking telling everyone to get a move on. Chesca vaulted onto Star's back and she began to canter, leading the way back to the barn.

"A pirate queen came to Howth and her simple wish was a place always be set at the table, ready for a person in need," she whispered.

She held her arms up to the morning sun and let her hair fly, imaging herself to be a pirate queen. "Fair play to you, Grace." Chesca said. "I bet you never did camps either."

*She never did...*whispered Wind.

"Grace defied her father but lived out her dreams."

*That's not the moral of the story, wait...there's more to it...*Wind said, but Chesca was cantering so fast now the words slipped by her.

Chapter 4

Dust clouds rose around the stamping hooves. The animals pushed through the farm gate into the yard, jostling for position and found their way into the barn.

Within seconds the chaos had subsided and peace had descended. They tucked into their breakfast, slurping, crunching, and licking. There is nothing as beautiful as breakfast in a barn.

A breeze moved through shafts of dusty light. The cobwebs in the upper windows, the sweet smell of hay in the loft, the limestone walls and aging, creaking oak doors, the birds cooing in the loft; this was the place they called home. In winter the Kerry cows slept in a tidy row, each separated by a plank hanging from the rafters by chafed rope. Pig and Donkey shared a stall. Malley, of course, had the biggest stall in the barn. Beside him was a tack room and office where Ma planned all the details of life on the farm: the bookings for the pony treks, riding lessons, the vet's visits, orders for feeding and the blacksmith—down to the last hot-fired shoe. A dusty old clock kept everyone on time with a loud tick-tock.

Chesca took out the grooming brushes. She picked up a soft body brush, looked at Tinker, a thick-coated Shetland covered from head to hoof in muck, and picked a hard brush instead. She'd need some elbow grease for this job.

"You little mucker," she talked to him like a best friend, "did you ever hear the story about the pony that rolled himself into a bog and couldn't get out for ten hours?" She worked the brush in a circle over his coat. "The firemen had to lift him out with a crane." Tinker snorted and kept on eating. The dust rose in the air, landed on her thick black hair and lightly dusted her cheekbones.

Ma walked out of the feed room, stirring a bucket of barley. "Your dad said you're putting music to your practice?"

"Wait 'til you see what I've put together. No silly old camps needed here. Maybe I could do a little show for you and Da?"

"No trick riding Ches, no dangerous stuff, OK?"

"I won't get hurt. I have Wind on my side." She thought it was time her mother understood the truth.

"I can do extraordinary things with my friends, and Malley said…"

"Your Aunt Dena said we should give up on the riding altogether, sell the whole place and retire to the country." Ma kept on stirring the large tin bucket. "She said, at your age you need to join the clubs and I think she may be right. Wouldn't you *like* to learn different things, instead of always being dirty, mucking out, grooming and sweeping?"

"Aunt Dena, Aunt Dena," Chesca said quickly, "what would she know? She doesn't even like kids. I think Da was right when he said you shouldn't listen to her," Chesca banged the brushes clean, causing a big dust cloud around her. "He said not to listen to a word out of her mouth. Aunt Dena knows nothing, absolutely nothing, about farms. Especially this farm—only a rare creature can appreciate this farm."

Ma took the ladle from the bucket and looked at her with a sideways glance. "Well, you're a rare creature, that's for sure," she said with a gentle sigh.

"Da said, if Aunt Dena behaved a little nicer, she would have found that husband she keeps looking for. He said men aren't as stupid as she thinks. He said, most men can see right through her."

"Enough of that kind of talk. A woman's entitled to find a good husband. I did, and I promised your granny, right before she died—may she rest in peace—that I would look out for my sister, always and forever." Her mother paused and seemed to ponder the bucket. "Even if it's hard sometimes, Ches, you don't give up on family."

"Talking of women. Did you ever hear the story about Grace O'Malley, a pirate queen that came to Howth and kidnapped the earl's grandson from the castle?"

Ma stood in the breezeway and looked out between the huge barn doors.

"The bold and brave Grace O'Malley. That's not all she did. I've been meaning to tell you about Grace, all about her."

Chesca entered Malley's stall and shut the half door but watched Ma scratch Polly's ear. Polly raised her head and leaned into her hand.

"How come I never heard of her before?" Chesca asked.

"Well...you won't find a brave woman like Grace in the school books. Sure the historians didn't know what to make of her. She was different."

"I'm different," Chesca said.

"Yes, Ches," Ma smiled at her, "and I have a feeling you will make the history books."

Chesca tried to hide her smile. "So, she's a forgotten pirate queen."

"She's a legend, her story being passed down over time by storytellers."

"I think she was great. Could you make me a cloak like hers, with rubies and emeralds?"

Ma stopped scratching Polly.

"I want to ride a golden horse, like Grace did. I want to ride Malley, across the mountains and into the seas." Chesca took a riding whip off the wall and lunged into the breezeway, slicing the whip through the air. "I want to be Chieftain of the East Mountain."

Malley looked at her, he stopped eating—a sparrow dove from a beam above them and there was a magical swirl of straw, oat husks and dust throughout the barn as Wind swept in through the doors—then he returned to his food.

Ma sat in her director's chair and slowly rubbed her forehead.

"I have my hands full here," she said. "Now would you get going, or there'll be no work done today."

"But, Ma…"

"Don't worry, I'll sort out your cloak," she said, rising from her chair. "Every chieftain needs a cloak."

Chapter 5

Mr. Davis, the baldie banker, arrived at precisely three o'clock. He drove a large Range Rover into the yard and slammed the car door. He wore a brown suit and he straightened his tie before he banged on the front door. He held a legal envelope in one hand and his briefcase in the other.

Da paced the kitchen, stoked the fire, and opened the front door.

"This won't take long," Mr. Davis said, as Ma offered him a seat beside her at the kitchen table. She sifted through a stack of bills, notices, and deeds as if she had lost something. Mr. Davis scratched the top of his shiny head and glanced over the rims of his glasses at Chesca. She glared right back at him. Something about him gave her the creeps.

"Go to the barn, Chesca," Ma said. "Get the hens into the coop, and the ducks need to be fed."

Going to the barn, Polly at her heels, she remembered she had left Mouse behind and turned back.

"Between taxes, back taxes, increased insurance and over-extended loans, there is no good news here," Mr. Davis said. Chesca ducked under the open kitchen window. Kneeling, she rubbed Polly's ear and listened as hard as she could.

"We can work something out," said Da. "If the weather holds we should have a great summer season. The milk's been selling first rate."

"Mr. O'Brien," said Mr. Davis, like a strict schoolteacher. "This is not a question of milk and pony rides. You must understand. I'm here on behalf of the bank to give your final notice. If your August payments aren't made in full, the bank will move to repossess."

Chesca peeked into the kitchen careful not to be seen.

Ma stopped searching through papers, and stared at him, puzzled, the way a child does when she doesn't understand.

"Over my dead body," she said with an unusually harsh tone.

Polly began panting nervously. Mouse appeared from a little hole in the wall. She looked shaky and her cheeks were pale. Chesca put her finger to her lips and kneeled back down under the window.

"Shush," she whispered, and put Mouse in her pocket.

"Mrs. O'Brien," Mr. Davis said, "my advice would be to sell the farm, sell it now, before the bank takes it. You'll get a good price for it. You'd be left with enough money to find a moderate home, maybe even a small farm in the country."

"Sell it? Was he mad?"

"We could never do that Mr. Davis, you see…" Ma said.

Da stood up. "No," he said. "We'll find a way. We always do. The O'Briens have been here for generations."

"Well then, good luck," said Mr. Davis. "I've given you the necessary papers from the bank. I hope to see you before August." There was a shuffle of feet and chairs.

Chesca spun around and followed Polly who was galloping to the barn. She flung open the barn doors, causing the animals to jump. She got to Malley's door as the first tears began to sting her eyes.

"You won't believe it," she said, catching her breath.

"What is it Chesca?" said Malley. He stood rigid.

The animals gathered. Rooster jumped down from the loft. Pig stood on Donkey's back and opened his stall door. They came around Malley's stall and looked out the barn doors as Mr. Davis drove out of the yard. Wind blew behind him and the gate rattled against the wall.

"What happened?" Malley said. He arched his neck, looked at her hands that were shaking and swung his head back in the direction of Mr. Davis.

"See that banker man? He wants to take the land."

"Is that a fact?" said Malley.

"You can't take a farm, silly," said Donkey laughing, but stopped when everyone looked at him with wide eyes.

"He said the banks will own the farm by summer's end."

The hens began their about-to-panic clucking. She watched Malley. There was a flicker of anger in his eyes. Maybe he'd break down the door and go after him. Maybe he should. He definitely should.

"We should stop him, now, before it's too late," she said. A loud clucking broke out.

"Calm down," said Malley, but the hens were getting louder.

Mouse started crying. "What will become of us?"

"Stop! Stop this mayhem," Malley said, his eyes darting from one animal to another. Then he looked at her. "What did your father say?"

"He said...well, he said the O'Briens had survived before and they'll survive this, or something to that effect."

Owl hooted from the loft.

"There you are, then," said Malley, as if that solved everything. "Your mother and father will find a way. Don't fret, Ches."

The animals looked to each other. Chesca could tell by the way Turkey held his wings out that he was nervous. Pig had his head between his legs and looked as confused as she was.

Malley stamped his hoof, drawing every eye back to him. "Now, let's understand why. Why does the money man want our land?" He looked at her sharply. "Throughout history there come challenges in all sorts of ways. We pull through. Always have, always will. Hens to the coop, cows to bed, and girls, chew, make that good milk great. We need to look sharp. There's work to be done."

"Is he an Amadan?" Donkey said to Malley. "Is he stupid?"

"This one is not," Malley said. "He's a different breed," Malley squinted at the driveway as if Mr. Davis was still there, "he comes with paper in his hands and the law on his side."

Chapter 6

t dinner that evening a heavy silence hung in the big old kitchen. Chesca set the table and filled each glass with milk.

"Do you remember, Claire, when we went to the fair in Carlow, when we were just newlyweds?" Da stood watching the milk flow into the glass then he served the dinner, spooning spuds onto each plate.

"I most certainly do," Ma said, "we won first prize in the dairy tasting competition." She ran a hand over her hair.

"That set us apart from the rest of them, especially for our great milk," he said. "They may be Kerry cows, but it's the Howth limestone land and sea air that won us that trophy, and every one since." Da banged his fist on the table like a gavel. "We'll be all right love, don't you worry."

"I know we will," Ma said.

He reached across the table and gently patted her hand. Chesca looked from one to the other, like watching a slow game of tennis.

"And now what?" she said, and shoved her plate to the middle of the table. "And now, what are we going to do?"

They turned as if seeing her for the first time.

"That bully banker said he was coming to take the farm."

"Chesca," Ma said, "I told you not to be listening to the adult conversations."

A tear stung her eye and she rubbed it away. An angry one, another angry tear was coming up, right behind it.

"Oh Ches," Ma sighed and eased her plate back. "We may have to sell something. I'm not sure what yet. Something to pay some bills. But nobody will force us to sell the farm, as long as I have a breath in my body." Chesca believed that, but what could they sell?

"That's enough of that now," Da said. "No more talk of selling farms."

They ate in silence. An occasional whinny could be heard from the meadows and a speckled lark sang its last song of the day. They watched Bamper, their loyal stable hand, ruddy-cheeked and slightly limping, letting the cows out to graze. The lead black and white cow ambled down the cobbled driveway, followed by the rest of the girls, swinging their tails while pulling and chewing at the grassy verge.

"If we could sell the formula for having such happy cows, we could pay off *all* the bills," Chesca said.

Da kept his eyes on the cows.

"Ah, yes," he said, "but you can't sell that, there's no price to happiness."

"No, but what if we did something different—unique? We should bottle our cow's happiness. Imagine Da...tall slim bottles with Maureen, our best cow, smiling on the front, the milk creamy with orange sparkles on the top, brimming over with bubbles."

"What?"

"With sparkles on top, Da."

He looked away from the window. "You have some imagination child," he said.

"Is that another way of saying you don't believe me? I've had teachers and parents say…'Chesca, dear, you have a wild imagination' or 'aw Chesca, you're away with the fairies.' Another way of saying they didn't believe a word of it. But Da. Maybe milkshakes are the answer."

He pushed the pile of paperwork from the table into a drawer and shut it. "No need for you to concern yourself, love. I'll find the answer."

Ma stood up and went to sit by the fire. She bent down and added a peat log; it smoldered then burst into flames. She massaged her temples, letting her long brown hair free. It folded in waves around her shoulders. She looked pale.

"Why don't you go to bed, I'll be up in a while. It's been a long day sweetheart and I've a headache," she said.

"Grand, I'm off to bed then. I've reading to do. Research on my show."

Ma looked over at Da but he had his hand under his chin, gazing out the window.

"I was thinking Ches," Ma said. "For your twelfth birthday, I'd like to throw you a little party, invite the other barns, the farmers and their families, Mrs. Dillon, the Murphy's—you know—our *friends*."

"Your friends Ma, not mine. I'd prefer a new bridle, a big one that would fit a large stallion." Chesca kissed her father goodnight and was happy her mother dropped the subject. She did look tired.

Chesca jumped into bed and wrapped the duvet around her. The shelves on either side were packed tight with books, candles, pictures of the animals, rosettes from shows and rallies, and trophies from pony club games from all over Ireland. There was a time, before she became a trick rider, before she changed from riding in tight circles to riding upside down, that she attended the shows. That was before Pig Senior died.

Her leather covered diary and silver pen lay on the cushion of the window seat overlooking the orchards. White drapes were pulled back on each side. On a fine day she could look past the apple trees to the sea, to the dancing waves. She could listen to Wind singing in the trees.

She whispered to Mouse, "They have to sell something, Mouse. I hope they don't have to sell the tractor. I love that tractor."

She picked up the book that Ma had given her for her birthday when she was eight. It was her favorite book and she referred to it often, *A Magical Horse Show.* She turned to the middle pages, double pages of a color picture. A horse as black as ink stood on his hind legs in a full rear, his front hoof stretching towards the stars. His wild eyes seemed to be looking right at her, as if trying to tell her something. She ran her finger over the outline of the horse, trying to bring the horse to life, and see what he would do next in his magical world.

She imagined he galloped into the arena, showing his audience his skill of speed and agility, side stepping and holding his hooves high, prancing and arching his neck, until the people clapped and cheered for more to the sound of drums and castanets, while the lights shone on his silky coat and made him glisten. Nothing would have made her happier than to be pulled into his world and see the magical horse show. She imagined it would be spectacular.

There was a soft knock on the door. Mouse tucked herself down and hid under the duvet as Ma entered the room, her sewing basket in her hand. Chesca sat up, put the book to one side and pushed her hair behind her ear.

"You asked about Grace O'Malley," Ma said.

"I like her. She was a great girl altogether. Did she have to deal with greedy bankers?" Chesca said, and handed her a hairbrush. Ma sat beside her and began brushing her hair.

"Oh, she dealt with bankers, captains, hangmen and queens." Ma tucked the blanket around her. "She left a legacy you know? Tomorrow I'll tell you a very special story. I'll find that book all about her. There is so much folklore and fact mixed together. I'll tell you everything, it's important for you to know. There are many people—fishermen and farmers, Howth people...well, they believe she is sailing still."

"Please tell me. Don't miss a detail."

"I want to start working on your cloak. We have time tomorrow."

Chesca stared past her mother and imagined riding Malley. He stretched his hind legs, reared, struck the air, then galloped across the rippled sands and out to the edge of the Irish Sea. Her cloak flew out behind her, like a pair of wings, sparkling and snapping. She imagined a flash of fire and light, Star dancing by the shine of the moon, her star as white as snow, and an audience of ten, no hundreds, thousands even, all clapping, because they finally realized the talents of her friends, the extraordinary magical ways of them. Mary Murphy was telling the girls in school, her socks pulled up to her knee, her hair in two braids and her glasses perched on her nose, tartan kilt with the shiny pin holding it closed near the end, everything in place, telling all the enchanted girls about the most amazing show anyone had ever seen. Finally, everyone would know she was not crazy.

"Maybe I could wear my cloak?" she said, "for the show."

"What show?" Ma rubbed her temple again then leaned over and kissed her daughter on the forehead.

"The show I'm going to do…for you and Da."

"That's right Ches, don't worry. Everything will be just fine."

Chapter 7

The smell of buttered toast woke Chesca. Sitting up and stretching, she felt the sun shining through the window onto her face and slowly she smiled. She rolled over and tickled Mouse's toes, then jumped out of bed and got dressed.

"You just can't beat Ma's breakfast," said Mouse, yawning. She let the breakfast aroma fill her little pink nostrils then scrambled into Chesca's pocket.

Chesca slid backwards down the banister, landing lightly.

"What's this?" she said.

Da was towering over the frying pan, cracking eggs.

"Quiet, child, your mother is still sleeping. I thought *we* could have breakfast then feed the barn." He stirred the eggs around the pan.

"Still sleeping?" said Chesca.

"Well," he said, taking a gulp of orange juice, "today she needs an extra hour. She was away with the fairies when I got up." He poured steaming tea into a mug. "She had a headache last night," he said. "We can feed the barn, you're old enough." He spooned sugar into the tea, then turned quickly, and knowing the house so well, caught the toast as it flew out of the toaster.

"I might get the mixes wrong," said Chesca.

"You know what the animals need," he said. "Sure you're a big girl now that you're nearly twelve. Your mother won't be long. He winked at her and walked out the door. Chesca tried to remember what the oldest horse in the barn, Comet, took in his oats. Was it calcium or iron?

"Da, when can I ride Malley?" she shouted after him, but he was already halfway to the barn. She ran after him.

Dear old Bamper in his worn jeans and patched jacket was busy at work. He moved quietly from stall to stall, tossing the straw and building the horses' beds ever so evenly. He was nearly as tall as her father; grey, older, more weather-beaten. He came every morning and worked silently in the barn, the dairy, out in the meadows and fields.

"How's the hay coming along, Bamper?" said Chesca.

Bamper blinked and nodded, his way of saying all was well. Her dad had the buckets out and was pouring hot water into a feeding vat. Chesca scooped rolled oats and beet pulp into tin buckets.

"Two scoops of oats for Star, with love," she said, mixing the grain with a huge ladle. "Two scoops for Tinker, with some kindness and a pinch of humor," she laughed.

"That's my girl, now you have it. I'm off to the dairy to milk the cows." He pulled his brown tweed cap down over his forehead. He walked outside, climbed up and started the finicky old tractor. It belched black smoke that rose in the morning air, and then it seemed to hiccup. Revving it up, he drove out of the yard.

After she had filled the last trough, Chesca went to the doorway to call the animals home, like Ma. She cupped her hands to her mouth then changed her mind and walked to the top of a hill near the orchard. A breeze rippled through the tops of the apple trees. Again she cupped her hands.

"'Hup," she shouted, but there was no power in her call, not like Ma's. She climbed the fence, and took a huge breath of fresh air, and from the pit of her stomach called them home.

"HUP, HUP, HUP." Her new voice seemed to rise from her belly to the top of her head. Mouse ducked. Chesca's call echoed around the Brandy Banks. She returned to the barn and opened the doors as wide as she could.

"I think they're coming!" she shouted to Bamper, delighted at the distant rumble. And come they did, galloping, skidding, snorting and squealing, into the farmyard.

Rooster was last. "For you, Chesca," he said. A painting under his wing dropped to the ground as he flew into the barn.

"Another beauty for the collection," Chesca said, rolling out a painting of the mountain by moonlight. "I hope you signed it." She climbed to the loft and placed the painting carefully in her secret hidey-hole. She had a mounting stash of canvases—all of Rooster's artwork.

"If you don't mind me asking," he said, flying up to the loft, "when did you take over Ma's job?"

Chesca climbed down the ladder. The horses began slurping and chewing.

"Hold on," Rooster said, jumping down from the loft and looking around for Ma. "You made breakfast, too?"

"I most certainly did," Chesca blew him a kiss and gave him a little rub on his crown.

Malley looked up from his trough. "Where is Ma?"

"I'm going to give her breakfast in bed and fresh flowers." Chesca grabbed the clippers and skipped to a tune in her head, snapping her fingers.

"She's sleeping," she sang back to Malley, on her way out the door.

Malley watched from his stall as she clipped pink roses from her garden.

"Sleeping?" he said.

Chapter 8

a?" Chesca felt the stillness of the house. "Ma, are you up?"

The kitchen was empty, the dishes still piled up from breakfast. Chesca shouted up the stairs, "You taking the day off?"

The cuckoo jumped out of the old grandfather clock. 8:00 am, long past the feeding hour.

Chesca took the stairs two at a time and pushed open her parents' bedroom door. Her mother still slept, curled up under the goose down comforter. She walked into the bedroom to go to her, when something caught her eye.

Hanging on the wardrobe in front of the mirror was a beautiful green velvet cloak. The sunlight hit off its rubies and emeralds. Its clasp was made of gold. A small silver sword was sewn inside it, partially hidden in the lining. Chesca took the cloak from its hanger and wrapped it around her shoulders. It felt comfortable. She put her face up to the morning sun and felt its warmth. She let her hair out of its ponytails and it fell around her shoulders. Only the sword felt cold and out of place. She pulled it out, facing the mirror.

"Grace O'Malley, the Pirate Queen, by land and by sea," she said, and sliced the air. Again the sun caught the rubies and there was a glint of red light.

"I love it," she said.

Ma slept.

"Hey, sleepyhead," Chesca moved toward the bed.

"Ma?" She kneeled down and brushed the hair from Ma's peaceful face. She gave her a little nudge.

"Ma?"

Nothing.

"Wake up, lazybones," Chesca whispered. She could feel the warmth of Ma's body and smell her sweet peachy scent, but she refused to wake.

"Ma," she whispered.

"Ma, stop joking." She could feel the sting of tears. "MAMMY."

Nothing.

"DA," she screamed and tried to open the window, but it was stuck. She banged the sash with her fist and pulled it open. Tears were blinding her. She remembered he was in the dairy.

"MALLEY!" she cried.

There was a crack and splintering of wood as Malley kicked his stall door open. The hens squawked and Pig squealed as they jumped out of Malley's way. They galloped out of the barn and stood under the window. Polly was racing through the gate, barking in frenzy.

"What's wrong, what's wrong?"

Chesca leaned out the window, her arms outstretched, no words to explain; her vision blurred by the tears. Donkey brayed loudly in circles, a white loud blur.

Bamper had heard her and moved quickly for an old man. Crossing the yard, he looked up at her.

"She won't wake up, she won't wake, and she's not moving," Chesca cried. She could hear Bamper climbing the stairs.

He took one look at Ma.

"Sweet, Jesus," he said. "I'll go for your Da, and the ambulance. I'll call the ambulance. You stay with her, Chesca."

Then he was gone.

She could hear the tractor now, the squeal of brakes, the pounding of her father's steps. He took the steps two by two. He burst into the bedroom. His face ashen, he looked at her mother, then he picked her up in his arms.

"You'll be all right, my love," and in the same breath, he shouted and cursed. "Where's the damn ambulance?"

He carried her down the stairs and out the front door, and Chesca followed him. The siren screaming and wailing as the ambulance came into the yard, the noise of it gave her a jolt.

"Everything will be grand," he repeated, stuck on the same line, over and over.

The ambulance pulled up at the front of the house and the doors sprung open. Two paramedics scrambled out and pulled out the stretcher. They wore starched navy uniforms and looked strangely out of place, Chesca thought. The ambulance was unnerving her.

"Bamper, close the gate after us," her dad said, sternly. "And Bamper, call Aunt Dena. Her number is by the phone." He laid Ma down on the stretcher and helped place a blanket over her.

"I'm coming with you," Chesca cried, trying to hold her hand.

"You stay here. I'll call you as soon as I can. Be a good girl for Aunt Dena. Promise."

"Aunt Dena? Da, I'll be fine on my own," she said.

One of the paramedics placed an oxygen mask over her mother's mouth and pushed the stretcher back into the ambulance.

"I'll be back as soon as I can," said Da, not taking his eyes off Ma. He looked scared. Chesca shivered.

The paramedic slammed the doors shut. The ambulance drove away from the house, past the barn and out the gate. The sirens began to wail. The animals watched. Chesca stood alone in the middle of the yard.

Chapter 9

ulling up a bale of hay, Chesca sat down beside Malley. "How bad can a headache be?" she said.

Nobody answered. The clock on the wall ticked and tocked. Through the open doors they could see Bamper heave the gate shut.

The metal bolt clanged against its cradle. Like a church bell, it rang around the mountain. CLOSED.

There was silence; only time ticked. Nothing moved. The afternoon crept in and a troubled energy lingered around the farm. By late afternoon black clouds had gathered around the mountain. Finally, Rooster took out his brush and painted the silhouette of Chesca sitting on the bale of hay, her chin resting in her hand, and Malley standing behind her. They gazed out towards the mountain and the green, brooding ocean. Wind was picking up, in little gusts, promising to get stronger.

She couldn't move off the hay. She felt an unusual drumming in her heart. What if her mother never came home? Mouse had been shaking in her pocket for the last hour. She needed to comfort her. She would—Ma would come home, she felt sure. She would be home tomorrow.

She looked up at Malley. He held his proud head high and looked at the gate.

"I don't ever remember the gate being closed," he said.

Chapter 10

 black convertible stalled at the gate and honked. Every eye in the barn was on the car. A woman stuck her head out the window.

"Man," she said, pointing her white-gloved finger at Bamper. Again the woman tooted her horn and called out the window. "Man. Man who phoned me." She wagged her finger at Bamper as he pitched the hay bales into the loft.

"Aye," Bamper said, dropping the pitchfork and turning.

"Come and open the gate," she said, "For God's sake, can't you see I need help?"

"That," said Chesca, "is Aunt Dena."

There was an uneasy gabble from the hens.

"Brace yourself, Mouse," said Chesca. "This one will frighten you."

The car skidded on the smooth cobblestones and jerked into the yard. Aunt Dena parked in front of the house. The car seemed to spit her out. She half fell out, half jumped. She composed herself, running her hands down her cream suit. She was beautiful, polished, with glossy brown hair pulled back in a neat twist.

"Frances-ca," Dena shouted in a singsong voice, -ca, -ca, -ca, echoing in the treetops. A flock of starlings flew from the tree. She looked around the yard. "Oh my God, it stinks." She held a hanky to her nose. Everyone watched her, bewildered.

She slammed the car door and stepped over a puddle. She looked up to the dark skies. A sparrow dove past her as he made his way back to the barn. She swatted at it with her purse, still holding the hanky to her nose.

"Strange dance," said Donkey.

"I don't think this one's a dancer," said Pig. Polly jumped up.

"No, Polly!" said Pig, but it was too late. Polly was running out the door and toward Aunt Dena, wagging her tail, her ears flattened in her best smile, always the one to greet people.

"Polly!" said Chesca, running after her.

Dena took one look at Polly and clutched her handbag to her chest. Polly leaped to give her one of her welcome-to-the-farm kisses. Then Aunt Dena did the unimaginable; she drew back her leg, let it fly and kicked her, catching Polly in the belly. Polly howled. Winded and crying, she limped back to the safety of the barn.

Chesca stopped, stunned, in the middle of the yard.

The doors of the barn slammed shut. There was a bang and clatter from inside. The iron bolt was shut in place. Chesca turned to see who could have done it. It must have been Bamper. She could hear Malley thrashing against the doors to get at Dena. She could feel his fury. A high-pitched whinny rang out; he was warning Aunt Dena, calling her a witch and was roaring something about, no one had *ever, never ever,* harmed the animals of this farm. He rammed the barn doors.

Chesca thought about letting him out, but remembered her promise to her father.

"I will not be attacked by a stinking mutt," Dena said. She fixed a strand of hair and checked her French manicure.

There was chaos in the barn.

Aunt Dena took no notice.

"Attack?" Chesca said. "She was just..."

"Yes, attack, Frances-ca." She waved at the luggage in the back seat of the car. "Now, take my bags to the house, young lady."

Chesca could feel Mouse shaking in her pocket.

"Don't worry Mouse, she won't be here long. Not if Malley gets out, anyway."

"Who are you talking to?" said Aunt Dena.

"I'm talking to my friend, Mouse."

"What mouse?"

Mouse trembled, popped up, jumped out of Chesca's pocket and ran. Dena froze.

"What a disgusting little rodent. I've never seen such a fat one," she said. She grabbed at her handbag and swung it after Mouse, but Mouse was already in her house in the hole in the wall.

"Don't, you, ever, touch my friends," said Chesca. She could feel her cheeks redden, "and Aunt Dena, if Malley smashes the door down, you're in for it." She kicked a tin bucket out of the way. It clanged and tumbled on the cobblestone yard, and she reluctantly went to get Dena's bags.

"Now that," said Dena, "is not very ladylike. And whoever Malley is, he does not scare *me*." Dena was looking around for Mouse.

"He should scare you," Chesca said. "He's from a long line of warriors—of *chieftains in fact,* and because the last person he ran off this mountain had a long, hard recovery in Dublin hospital. Word has it, the Amadan still doesn't know what hit him."

Aunt Dena was at the front door now. She turned and looked at her, shook her head then pushed the door open and sniffed. Chesca dragged the large suitcase behind her. If her dad were not so upset right now she would have kicked the suitcase too. But something about Dena gave her the chills while rousing her curiosity.

"And just who is this Malley fellow," said Dena, "Some rogue stable hand?"

"He's the bravest stallion in the whole of Ireland. And I've never seen him so angry."

"A horse," Dena smirked. "A chieftain? This *is* the funny farm."

The phone rang in the hall.

Da. Chesca dropped the bag, but Aunt Dena rushed ahead of her and beat her to the phone.

"Yes, Thomas, I have arrived," she said, smiling a beautiful warm smile at Chesca, shifting her gaze to the stairs and around the hall. She sniffed and checked her nails. Her tailored cream jacket, an expensive wool, fit snugly around her narrow waist, her leather boots shiny brown.

"What did the doctors say?" Dena studied her nails. "I see. Oh. That's not good."

"Let me talk to Da!" Chesca said. She reached for the phone, but Dena turned her back to her. Chesca jumped in a circle to get the phone but Dena held it and turned.

"Well, let's hope for some good news in the morning," Dena said, glancing over her shoulder at Chesca. "Oh, and Thomas don't worry about Frances-ca, she'll be just fine." She hung up.

"I wanted to talk to him," Chesca shouted. "What did he say, what's wrong with my mother? Why didn't you let me talk to him?"

"Control yourself, I told your mother. I warned her this would happen. My poor, poor sister."

"What are you talking about?"

From a little hole in the wall Mouse called up to her. Chesca looked down. All she could see were Mouse's eyes, terror-filled, in the black depth of the hole.

"Frances-ca," Dena said. She started to place her hands on Chesca's shoulders but folded her arms instead. She walked into the kitchen and from her bag took a cigarette and lit it.

"She had a brain hemorrhage." She blew a stream of smoke into the air. There was only the sound of her breathing, as they stood looking at each other. Not a bird sang nor the Wind blew.

"I'm not a bit surprised," she said slowly.

"What? What did you tell her? You told her she would have a brain hemorrhage?"

Dena shifted her gaze from the peeling paint walls to her. "I told her not to marry a farmer, but she never listens, your mother. Look at this place, it's no wonder."

Chesca watched this woman, this aunt that was supposed to love her. Aunt Dena ran her fingertips over the stovetop, making sounds of disgust.

"Is she going to get better?" Chesca said.

She stopped and stared at her again. "My whole life, I have tried to help your mother, but she always does it her way."

"Is she?"

"The doctors are doing all they can." She flung the words over her shoulder circling the kitchen, opening and shutting the cabinet doors. "You know I told her," slam, slam, "I told her to sell this place. When was the last time your mother had a manicure, huh? I can tell by the look of the place that you are of no help to her, at all. Now if you were my child, things would be different—very different," she turned sharply and looked at Chesca, pointing the cigarette at her. "And that father of yours. Him and his cows and his green acres, and his sweet sickening romantic ways, well what good is it now?" Dena looked out the kitchen window. She sniffed. Thunder echoed across the East Mountain. The rain came slowly, gathering momentum 'til it pelted the roof and windows, and then there was a heavy silence.

"You know," said Dena, looking back to the paint peeling off the ceiling, "in my business, in the interior design business, we call this place a tear-me-downer, kind of the opposite to a fix-me-upper, and that's what I'd do with this place if it were mine."

"I'm not your child," said Chesca firmly. "And thank God it's not your place." She ran to the hallway and sat down on the bottom stair with a thump, feeling her chest tighten. She watched the rain form rivulets down the windowpane. Her hand slid on soft silk. She picked it up: her mother's green scarf. It lay where it had fallen just this morning. A tear trickled down her face. Chesca wiped it away before the rest of the dammed-up tears broke through. She put the scarf in her back pocket. If only she could turn the clock back to before the banker came. It was the baldie banker that gave her mother the headache.

Dena stood before her, looking down at her as another rumble of thunder crossed the skies.

"No, you're not my child." Dena ran a finger over her brow. "Let's just hope, dear Frances-ca...," she stepped past her on the way up to the guest room "...that your mother gets better soon."

Chapter 11

It was after dawn, after the feeding hour even, and strangely quiet. Chesca stood in the hallway and put her eye to the crack in the guestroom door. Her Aunt lay sleeping, her hair fanned around her peaceful face. She looked so much like her Ma. They were beautiful.

Owl hooted from the fir tree outside the bedroom window. Her Aunt woke with a sneeze. The dust motes drifted in the rays of light. He hooted again and flapped his wings then pecked on the window and jumped up and down before flying away and Chesca had to hold in the laughter. *Cheeky OWL.*

"Jesus, Mary and Joseph. I'm in hell," her aunt said. She looked at the alarm clock. It was 7:00 am. She flipped back the comforter and got up, her red silk nightdress falling like liquid around her legs. She picked up a large picture on the bedside locker. Her parent's wedding day. It was Chesca's favorite picture because it captured everyone, all her parent's friends and loved ones, gathered together on the steps of the church. Her dad had a big goofy grin on his face as he carried her Ma down the last steps of the church. Comet, three years old then with no grey around his muzzle, waited with the carriage to take them to their castle reception. Comet told her it was a magical day. Chesca wondered now if she would ever have a day like that: a day surrounded by friends. Then shook the thought out of her head. She didn't need them. She had everything she needed right here, on the farm, alive and kicking.

In the picture Ma looked delighted with herself in her pretty white dress, and there—there was Dena—standing behind the wedding party with her scowl. As Chesca spied, Dena tapped her fingernail on an image of Mrs. Dillon, standing in the crowd, smiling proudly, looking out from her rose colored glasses on the tip of her nose.

"What were you thinking, Sis? You could have had it all."

She muttered a few words.

Chesca heard heavy footsteps below in the kitchen and the smell of coffee, but couldn't stop spying on her Aunt.

She remembered once her aunt visiting during Christmas. She arrived dressed in a velvet skirt and red silk blouse with three parcels, a book on etiquette for Chesca, a monopoly game for Da, and a basket of beauty products including a certificate for a manicure and pedicure for Ma. Later, when Dena was gone, they all laughed so hard at their new gifts. Da held up the game and declared himself the new owner of a hotel, the Eiffel tower and he was out to buy the Tower of London. Ma leaned against the sink laughing. Da was in full theatrical form and Chesca loved this drama and fun, more than card night. She curtsied.

"And would the kind sir forgive this peasant child that has no..." she looked at her new book and slowly pronounced the word, eti-quette. This set her mother into another round of laughter and Ma jumped into the action of their family play.

"Be off with you both, and get ready for Mass, and dress well to compensate being seen with such an ugly matriarch." And she held the anti-wrinkle cream to her face with a smile. Now Da snorted and coffee spluttered everywhere and the three of them laughed and Chesca thought it was the best Christmas so far.

But then Ma wiped the table and said, "You know, she means well, that's the thing about my sister; she puts a lot of energy into downright insulting things, but she means well."

Dena walked out of view and returned from the closet wearing a brown cashmere suit, over a silk cream blouse, finished with a long strand of pearls. Then, sitting in front of a little antique vanity, she massaged cream into her neck and cheeks. She frowned as she touched a wrinkle, then a crow's foot.

"Lord, stop it, stop it with the grey and the aging and the lines." She looked to the mirror a little closer, spied one grey hair and pulled it, ran a finger over her brow. She turned to the picture.

"You should have listened to me, sister. You should have developed the land years ago. Because if you did it my way, you could have made a fortune, built yourself a house the size of Tara, and made Scarlett O'Hara look like a light weight." She pointed at the happy couple, "And it's far from Dublin hospital you'd be."

There was a loud outburst in the yard. Donkey was braying and Pig squealing for their breakfast. Dena went to see what was the commotion. Chesca quietly ran back to her room. Donkey had a mouthful of pebbles and fired them at her bedroom window. *Rat, tat, tat.*

She put her finger to her lips and signaled him to be quiet. There was a clop-clop of boots on the stairs.

"There's a mad donkey at the window, Thomas," said Dena. "THOM-AS."

Now Da was speaking from the kitchen.

The voices were muffled and she strained to hear his words. She got her jeans on and pulled on her boots. They were talking about Ma.

She did a practice kick to the air, and a karate chop then pulled her hair back, tied it in a pony and flung open her window.

Donkey looked up at her. "Where's breakfast?"

"Go to the Brandy Banks, call a meeting. I'll be there in a little bit," she said, and let the window slide shut with a bang.

"Come on, Mouse," said Chesca.

"I'll stay here," Mouse said.

"You're coming. I'm going to tell Da about the Polly abuse and the horrible things she said. Then Da will...," she kicked the air again, "kick her OUT."

She put Mouse in her shirt pocket and tiptoed down the stairs. Mouse was shaking and pointing to the cubby under the stairs, where the peat briquettes were kept.

"Let's just see what he says," whispered Mouse with a tremble.

Chesca felt sorry for poor Mouse. She hated conflict and got so worked up she shook for hours.

She nodded and moved lightly, squeezing into the peat cubby. The kitchen door was ajar. She could hear Aunt Dena tapping her nails on the table.

"I have a twelve o'clock meeting, in the House of Design, Monday morning," she said. "It's work and it's important."

"You can cancel," her dad said.

"That daughter of yours, she could do with some discipline. She talks to a mouse. Now, that should stop. She's a little strange. You don't want people laughing at her."

"All Chesca needs is her mother back home."

Chesca could hear her father's heavy boots as he crossed the kitchen. A nasty smell of acidic nail polish remover drifted around the house.

"Well Thomas, I'd never be one for telling you how to run things, but she could do with some manners."

"You always tell people how to run things, Dena."

Silence.

Just tell her to go.

"Listen Dena, she needs all the support she can get."

"Yes, why don't you call on that bossy friend of Claire's, Mrs. Fillon?"

"It's Mrs. Dillon, and if it was my choice Dena, that's exactly what I'd do, but Claire always, always, puts family first, and you are her only family to call on. So Dena, could you help her out?"

Chesca pulled her knees closer to her chest. It was getting uncomfortable in the small space. She closed her eyes and tightened her fists. "No Da, just tell her to go," she whispered.

"I need to be with Claire." Da must have put his teacup in the sink with a clink. "Could you stay here until she comes home? Chesca will give you no trouble."

"We could work something out. How long?" Dena said.

"I don't know," Da said. "The doctors can't tell me."

"You know, I don't like farms," Dena said. "I hate the smell of them. I really can't stay long."

"For Claire, Dena. She'll be so happy when she returns and you are here." There seemed to be a long pause. Chesca held her breath.

"Of course for Claire, Thomas. Believe it or not, all I ever want is the best for my sister.

There was silence. Chesca could hear the larks outside. Ah Da, just tell her to go home.

"I could stay a week, maybe, help her out a little, but Thomas…"

"What?"

"Get rid of those noisy, stinking, animals."

Chesca thought she would laugh out loud. *A farm without animals?* She waited for her father to do the same.

"I'll tell Bamper to keep them down the meadows," he said, walking out of the kitchen, letting the door slam.

Chapter 12

Chesca tumbled out of the peat cubby and ran through the kitchen past her aunt, slamming the door behind her. Her father was on his way to the Jeep now, dressed in his Sunday suit and black shoes. Chesca came running out, her shirt flapping and her hair wild. He got in and shut the door.

"Ches, love, I didn't want to wake you." He looked pale and tired.

"I'm coming with you," Chesca said, about to jump into the jeep.

"No. It's no place for a child." He looked at the sun-dried rose that lay on the dashboard of the Jeep. "It's a dark place, not much joy there."

"Ma needs me too," Chesca said. "I can help."

"You'd do better here, at the barn." He turned away, releasing the hand brake and pushing the jeep into gear. "Hospitals can be gloomy."

Chesca pictured her mother in a dark room surrounded by wrinkled old doctors and dark spirits, swirling all around her—long boney fingers and green breath. She had heard that Dublin Hospital was older than the hills. She felt a cold shiver cross the back of her neck.

Da revved the Jeep.

"No funny stuff when I'm gone," he said. "Can you promise me? No galloping around the moors at midnight without tack. No trick riding. Just keep it normal. Can you do that for me, love?"

"What about the farm?" Chesca noticed an overnight bag on the passenger seat.

"Bamper will do the milking and feeding," he said. "I've cancelled all the rides and lessons. All you have to do is collect the eggs."

"But it's our busiest time. I can take care of the lessons. I can mind the horses." Chesca felt the tears well up. They stung at her and she angrily rubbed them away.

"Chesca," he looked away from her.

"I can do it. I can feed the horses, I can. We need the business now more than ever, Da. Let me take care of the horses and the riding lessons."

"Just be a good girl for your Aunt Dena."

"How?" said Chesca. "How will we keep the bank man away, stop him from selling the land?"

"Oh, now, sweetheart," he said. "Rest easy. Let me take care of things. I'll find a way. There's always a way, believe me."

He looked at her, but she thought he looked through her; his expression blank.

"I do. I believe you, Da," she said.

"I've never let you down."

"I know, Da."

"And I'll fix this, too."

Reaching out the window, he gently pulled a strand of hair behind her ear. "It's going to take time, sweetheart. Ma will get better and the farm will be back to its happy, busy self. Be strong."

Somewhere, someone had lost a green balloon and it floated high in the sky passing clouds and drifted out of sight.

"Oh," she remembered, "Ma will need this." She handed him the headscarf from her back pocket. It smelled of her mother's shampoo and of sweet summer timothy. He put it in his breast pocket.

"Good child, everything will be grand," he said. "And keep that bank stuff to yourself. We don't want anybody knowing our business, especially Aunt Dena."

"Aunt Dena...," Chesca said. She was about to tell him exactly what she thought of her aunt, but she was silenced by the sadness in her father's eyes. He revved the jeep.

"Listen, Chesca. What harm can she do?"

Chapter 13

ena sat upright in the leather chair by the phone in the kitchen. She snapped Ma's day planner shut when Chesca walked in. She wore fresh lipstick and smelled of the perfume Joy. It was 7:30 am.

"The smell, the old dog smell," said Dena, so coolly. "What can we do about it?"

"It's a farm," said Chesca.

"It's an awfully smelly farm."

"They usually are."

Chesca got a sweet, sickly whiff of perfume. "Something does smell odd," she said. Dena got up and walked behind Chesca.

"Such lovely hair." She took Chesca's long black hair and held it in a pony.

Chesca pulled to get free, but Dena tightened her grip for one second before she released it.

"I don't like it here," Dena said.

Chesca rubbed her head and snapped at her, "I don't like you being here."

"You're going to shape up," her Aunt said. "You'll attend camp at the Castle. It's what your mother wants for you."

"No, it's not," Chesca tried not to shout.

"It is," Dena blinked. She moved to the mirror over the fireplace and stood looking at herself. "She told me she wanted you to go to summer camp." She turned her head left, right, admiring her reflection.

"She didn't say that," said Chesca. "She said, *you said,* I should go."

"Yes...and your mother agreed with me, your mother always agrees with me."

"She didn't," said Chesca. *Did Ma say that? Had Ma agreed with her?*

Dena took a lipstick from her handbag and began twisting the top up in small precise movements. "She said she is so worried about you turning into a gypsy, or running away with the circus, all that jumping around and swinging from trees and standing on horses. She's sad and disappointed that you don't listen to her wishes. I mean talking to a mouse, and...and this place," she sighed, looking around her. "Lord knows she has her hands full."

"Ma said that?" Chesca suddenly felt cold.

"Mmm, humm," Dena leaned into the mirror as she applied a coat of bright red lipstick. "Probably part of what made her sick. All that worry." She smacked her lips together.

Chesca looked at the cornflakes in her bowl. She couldn't eat.

From the mirror Dena caught her eye and smiled.

"Now." She puckered her lips and smacked again. "The time has come to help your mother." She ran her finger over her brow, searching the mirror for any imperfections in her reflection.

"I suggest," she smiled to herself, "we do what we can to help her with this mess."

"She loves this house, just the way it is."

Dena turned abruptly from the mirror. "Do you really, really think, that any woman in her right mind would love living in this house?" Dena pointed to the ceiling and then to the curtains. "This house is a bit like yourself, it needs a fresh look. How you present yourself, and your home, is a window into your very soul." She was standing very near the hole in the wall and Chesca prayed Mouse didn't poke her head out.

"Your father, Frances-ca," she said, pointing at her, now, "is so much more interested in the dairy than his wife or his home. He's always going on about the cows this and the cows that. Moo-moo here and moo-moo there. Let me tell you something about women Frances-ca, and it won't be long before you'll be a woman, looking for a decent man. All women love beautiful things." Chesca recognized the blush on Dena's cheeks, but where her mother's were beautiful, these cheeks were angry. "No decent, God-fearing Irishwoman likes dusty, moldy old things, and it's time your father sat up and paid notice of what a woman really wants."

88

"I never heard her complain," Chesca said.

"Well, I did."

They eyed each other.

"I don't believe you," Chesca said.

Dena picked up the phone from its cradle on the side table by the fire and pressed some numbers carefully, without chipping her nails. With her back to Dena, Chesca opened the drawer of the kitchen table. The stack of bills, farm documents and tax information sat where her father had put them on the day Mr. Davis arrived. She looked around, and quietly dropped them into a waste paper bin.

"Sue," Dena said, "cancel all my appointments for next week. Get me the number of the local boutique. There's an emergency here in Howth that needs my immediate attention. Oh, and get my little red book, you know the one, my who's who of Dublin...and one more number...pest control."

Chapter 14

hesca took the waste paper bin and bolted out the door. Outside, she whistled sharply and Mouse came running out of the hole and jumped into her hand. She ran with the bin to the barn, threw open the double doors and went to the office. She kneeled down to the thick steel safe her father kept there, took the bundle of papers, stuffed them into the safe, and locked the door. As her dad said, the less Dena knows, the better.

"We need to keep her in the dark on everything, Mouse."

"She's really scary," Mouse looked like she was going to cry. "What's pest control?"

"I haven't the foggiest, Mouse. She's a confusing one, that's for sure." Chesca hid the key under a heart shaped rock. "How can she be Ma's sister?" She stroked a finger over Mouse's head. "I bet she was dropped on her head as a baby," said Chesca.

She stomped down Whispering Lane, jumping hard into puddles from the night's rain, letting the rainwater spray her jeans and boots. Big white clouds raced overhead and only a burst of sunshine occasionally broke through. Owl flew before her, hooting, letting the animals know she was on the way. The trees rustled, waving her on. Wind ran beside her.

Trouble, whispered Wind in the treetops, bristling... *trouble, trouble, trouble.*

"I'm not afraid of her," Chesca said. "Plain to see she can't find a good husband and is angry at Da because *he is a good husband.*

The animals were gathering around the cottage, waiting for her. Chesca ran toward them jumping over Babbling Brook. She caught her reflection, her long legs and her black hair flying behind her as she landed. "The spit of her," she said, kneeling down. "I'm the spit of Ma." She pulled her hair back from her face and looked into the reflection of the water, seeing her green eyes looking back and the natural upturn of her lips. Even when she was this sad, or angry with Dena, she looked as calm as her mother. People said graceful, others said beautiful. She frowned. The water gurgled over pebbles and mossy rocks. The grey skies were thick and heavy; the mountain silent.

When she looked up, Malley stood before her.

"What ails her, Chesca? Is Ma back home yet?" he said. Chesca recognized the kindness in his eye.

"What's the news?" Polly panted, wagging her tail, and jumping up to slobber Chesca with kisses, nearly sending her headfirst back into the brook.

Pig heard them and pulled his head out of a prickly gorse bush, where he'd been looking for mushrooms. He grunted and bucked, his behind tipping so far forward he somersaulted and landed on his back. Chesca would have commented on his gymnastic style, maybe even have done a somersault together, but images of her mother in the hospital in Dublin city stayed with her.

The hens began an excited clucking when they spied Chesca. Ah, the hens were always happy to see her, they all were, and she felt a new wave of tears spring up in her eyes, but blinked them back. The hens and Mouse would need her to be strong.

"Ma had a brain hemorrhage," she said.

All the animals moved closer together, around her.

"That's why there's no breakfast," Donkey brayed. "I knew it was bad. What's a hemorrhage?"

"When is she coming home?" said Star, not looking at all dramatic or diva-ish.

"Nobody knows," said Chesca, shaking her head. "Poor Ma. And, to make things worse, Aunt Dena wants all of you to stay away from the farm. A farm without animals. I mean...it's her that's strange, not me."

A bee buzzed around the hawthorn tree.

Chesca did a one-handed handstand and stayed that way. New blooms of heather had sprung up overnight and the yellow flower of the gorse had opened among the long thorns. The meadowlark sang his high-pitched tune. She looked at her upside down friends and them at her.

"I've to learn manners and take swim lessons, and this lesson, and that lesson, blah, blah, blah, and...she said Ma was disappointed in me." Her arm began to wobble slightly.

There was a loud squeal. "That's ridiculous! She's the proudest mother in all of Ireland," Pig said. "Don't listen to a word of it, the conniving, treacherous, troublemaker."

"Pig." Malley scolded.

Chesca let her legs touch the grass and stood upright. Her face was red and her hair was a mess.

"When does she leave?" said Turkey, hopping onto a branch above them looking left and right. He stood on his claw tips and glanced toward the mountaintop for any movement from a preying fox or a mad dog. He could see over Whispering Lane to the house. Now he would watch for the bad aunt.

On the upper cliff path, three girls on well-groomed ponies from the Murphy barn, galloped along the mucky trail, sending clods of soil and puddle water in all directions. Turkey turned his back on them, but Chesca saw them as they rounded the bend towards the Brandy Banks. The path wound above the fields on common land and they were permitted to ride there, but if they jumped the little fence onto the O'Brien land, she would tell them they were trespassing and to get off her land. She watched as they rode past them, urging their ponies faster, kicking them on with their polished black leather boots, heels to the side, straight back, hands giving with the movement of the pony's heads, just like they had been taught in their lessons every Saturday morning, around and around in circles, 'til it made your head dizzy. Just knowing about their lessons bored Chesca to tears.

They didn't look her way and she felt thankful for all her animals. They were loyal and loving and would never go around in circles, well, maybe Donkey but he enjoyed it, his way.

"Just how should we get rid of Dena?" she said and thought about the expression the 'spit of her'—about her mother and herself—and wondered how Ma and Dena could come from the same root?

Everyone stood in deep thought. A flock of starlings raced overhead. Wind blew wave over wave in the ocean.

"Maybe we could do a plain old fashioned run," said Turkey, jumping down.

"We'll run her right off the mountain," Pig said.

Chesca nodded. "That's what I thought...that horror show named Dena needs help out the gate."

"That's not like you," said Donkey, "the only time I see you mad is with those girls from the other barn, and I'm still not sure why, Chesca."

"Why, Donkey? Because they don't believe in magic. They don't believe in us, they don't even believe in their own magic. Look at them."

Three round rumps disappeared in the distance.

The sun broke through and shone on the cottage. Chesca turned back to Donkey. "They're always looking to see what we're doing. They don't believe they can do better themselves and they don't like being different. It's that simple and I'm not angry with them anymore. I'm sad for them. But this is different, Donkey. Dena kicked Polly, and wants to kill Mouse. She has bad in her and she's a liar," Chesca said, looking from one friend to another.

"Well," said Pig, "I say throw her in the slurry tank. That should do the job—or a manure burial is always a good one."

"Wait," said Malley, gazing out to sea.

Everyone looked at him and Chesca thought he was joking. Wait?

"What?" they all said.

"We have to wait."

"How can you say that, Malley? Why?" said Chesca. "Pig's right. Let's frighten the living daylights out of her and maybe she'll go home. Da only wants her here because she's supposed to be family. She hates it here. She hates Da...and me."

"And me," said Mouse, "she really hates me."

"Let's run her off, NOW," Chesca said, fiercely.

Everyone stared at her. The hens started clucking nervously.

Malley's deep voice soothed everyone. "But, this is Ma's sister."

Silence.

"We need caution. We need to be clever, calm." His words seemed to linger around the treetops. A mountain hare peeped out of the woods, looked around and bounced off through the ferns and through the stone wall.

"And this," said Pig, "coming from him-who-hung-the-butcher-over-the-cliff, until the man's apron strings could hold him no longer?"

"That was different, Pig," Malley said. "He wanted to steal the hens. Immediate action was called for."

Chesca watched him. He was so much calmer than yesterday that was for sure. Too calm. She wondered what had changed. Hardly the time for smelling the roses. This was war. Why was Malley not up in arms?

Turkey flapped his wings, scouting. A wild turkey can see an eye move or blink for a hundred yards. "So," he gobbled, "we can't run her off. But, nobody said her stay has to be a comfortable one."

"That's right, Turkey," said Chesca. "Let's call the spiders and birds. I bet they'll help. Owl has some wake-up call."

Owl hooted and a sign was sent across the mountain. Although Chesca didn't know exactly what Owl had said, she believed Owl was calling in help. She watched him fly from the tree. His huge wings flapped, stretched out and he soared towards the hilltop, over the heather and yellow gorse.

"Chesca, don't let the Dena one upset you," Malley said. "Come on, let's just imagine Ma home. It may all blow over. Picture it, Ma comes home, Aunt Dena leaves, Da sorts out the bank man. That's the plan."

Chesca shut her eyes. She should get back to the house. Maybe Ma was home already. In her mind's eye she saw her scooping out the oats and hot bran, dark tresses curled around her shoulders and her scarf around her head. Then Dena appeared in a cloud of dust and Chesca lost sight of her mother.

"Sorry, Malley, but as long as Aunt Dena is here, Ma is not."

Chapter 15

In the kitchen something was wrong. It felt empty. Chesca stood in the center and turned. The framed photographs of the horses, Pig and the Kerry Cows winning prizes at the country fair: gone. The house smelled of Pine Sol and bleach.

Mouse screamed. A mousetrap set for the kill lay just outside her house. She fainted, dropped like a coin in Chesca's pocket.

Chesca bent down and put a pencil on the trap and it snapped shut so fast it nearly took her nose off. She threw it across the room.

Dena was marching along the driveway now, her black Pashmina wrap draped over her head and flapping in the wind.

"Quick," Chesca said, but was talking to herself. Mouse was still out cold. She set off another trap by the stove and looked around the skirting boards. There was another tucked under the fridge and one beside a bookstand. Little bowls with brown pellets sat under chairs and along by the fridge.

"God, almighty…it's poison," Chesca said. "She's a murderer."

She ran upstairs to her bedroom taking the stairs two at a time. "Mouse, you have to stay here. Don't go out the door without me." Mouse sat back up in her pocket and she looked around them, her eyes as big as pennies.

The sheets on Chesca's bed had been changed from white to hideous bright pink with baby-blue polka dots. There was a poster of Barbie and Ken on the wall where her horse posters used to be.

"Barbie?" Chesca pulled the poster off the wall. "I hate Barbie!"

A tennis racket and a tube of balls lay on top of the new pink pillow. Chesca ripped the top sheet off and the tube hit the floor, scattering tennis balls everywhere.

She pulled open her drawer and stared. Her jeans were folded and labeled for each day of the week with a color coordinated top and ribbons for her hair. Her chaps were gone, replaced by tennis skirts and white tennis shirts. She kicked the closet door and it swung out in protest, and there it was: the puffiest, bluest, most ribbony dress you could imagine. She slammed the door.

"Never."

Something was missing. She ran into her parents' bedroom. The dust bunnies and the pile of old newspapers were gone. She rushed to the wardrobe and flung open the doors. She rifled through her dad's shirts and her mother's blouses. She reached up and ran a hand over the top shelf; just shoeboxes full of papers, her mother's camera and jewelry box.

"Oh, Mouse, where is it?" She pushed further into the wardrobe, the shirts brushing her face.

She was about to give up. It was dark and quiet; she could hear only the sound of her own breathing. Then a ray of sunshine lit the closet and a bit of green velvet caught her eye from the very back corner.

"Thank you, dear cleaners, whoever you are," Chesca said, and grabbed the cloak from its hanger and ran with it into her bedroom. She slammed the door. Leaning against it, she caught her breath.

Aunt Dena was in the house. Chesca could hear the click of her boots. Wind was banging against the window. It was the first time she heard the mantra and couldn't make head nor tail of it. "*Level-it, level-it, level-it.*" Her aunt was chanting away like she was possessed.

What in God's name does levelit mean?

Dena sang out from the bottom stair. "Where were you?"

"Collecting eggs," Chesca sang back from behind the door.

"You took all day to collect a few eggs?"

"The hens were busy. We had a meeting." Chesca realized her mistake.

"What meeting?" There was the click of heels climbing the stairs.

"Just joking. I was...cleaning. I was cleaning the coop". The heels stopped near the top of the stairs.

"Did you see your new dress?"

"I did," Chesca said, praying she didn't try to come in. She held the cloak in her arms. Mouse shook in her pocket. Chesca leaned harder on the door.

"Do you like your new dress?" said Aunt Dena.

Mouse held her paws up in prayer. "Please say yes," she squeaked.

"I...love it," Chesca said, but looked like she had eaten a sour drop.

"You do?" said Aunt Dena. She sounded close, too close. "And Frances-ca, what do you make of your room?"

"Seriously?" Chesca whispered to Mouse. "I hate it, I hate her, I..." Chesca could hear her dad's advice like a far off whisper, *"she just wants to play house,"* and Malley's, *"keep the peace."*

"Great, Aunt Dena, you have a wonderful way with a home," Chesca said, looking at the bed sheets, pretending to vomit.

"Wonderful," she paused. "Now take that bath." There was the shuffle of boots moving away from the door.

Mouse had begun to cry. "I wish Malley was here," she said.

"It's alright Mouse. Let's find a new hiding place," Chesca said, looking about the room.

"Are you talking to yourself?" Dena rattled the door. Chesca and Mouse stopped moving and breathing, but the door did not open, and her voice drifted as she went down the stairs.

"Talking to yourself, my, my," she said. "Oh Frances-ca dear, I'm looking for an old cloak of your mothers. The cleaners must have put it away but it would make good curtains for the kitchen. If you find it, let me know."

Chesca looked about the room. "Curtains. Good God. We must hide you precious things," she said. Below the nook was a cubby, with a wooden door. Chesca knelt and stashed the cloak. She placed an uncovered glass jar in the corner of the nook.

"When I'm gone, Mouse," she said, holding Mouse on the flat of her palm at eye level, "you must stay in the jar. Goodness knows how many traps she put around the house. "She's trying to trap us all. She's trying to control us and change us, but she won't. We won't let her, Mouse."

Dena was back in the kitchen. *Slam, slam, slam* the bang of kitchen cabinets and the table drawer.

"What's she looking for?"

"She wants to kill me," Mouse trembled.

They didn't hear the knock on the front door. If Chesca had, she would have received Jimmy Hickey standing bow-legged, with his eye patch on crooked, and his long hair tied in a pony.

Jimmy Hickey was testimony to the hardships of a fisherman's life. He looked beat up and rolled around on the high seas, yet he had come to deliver a basket of fresh fish, homemade bread, apple pie and jam. Mrs. Dillon from the village had put it together. The label read: "Chin up, Chesca. She'll be home soon."

She heard Aunt Dena slam the dresser shut, grab one of six new brooms she had waiting there, her emergency supply. She heard the door open, and Dena shout, "Vermin."

She put Mouse down and shut the cubby door then ran and looked out the bedroom window overlooking the farmyard, but missed Jimmy Hickey running out the gate. More than anything, she had missed an act of kindness from her mother's best friends.

Chapter 16

Chesca sat in her nook and looked up at the half-moon. She missed Ma. She picked up her pen and diary and doodled. The house was silent. She leaned her head against the cool window. Mouse sat in her lap. She seemed smaller and shakier, with a permanent look of worry etched in her brow. Chesca pulled the cloak around them. The green velvet shone in the light of the moon and the stones gleamed. Maybe, she thought, it would help her. Maybe it would protect them. The last thing her mother did before she… before she went to sleep…was work on the cloak. She wanted, needed, to see her mother, despite what her father had said.

Mouse curled up and looked at her.

"Tell us a story," she said, in need of distraction.

A breeze shook the treetops and they swayed gracefully, like ballroom dancers, but Wind said nothing and played with no one.

Chesca put her pen down.

"Ages ago, when I was seven," she said, rubbing Mouse's head, "on a cold day, the rain lashed the mountainside. I was cleaning the bridles by the fire. A traveling gypsy woman knocked on the front door, looking for hot milk for her baby. Ma took them to the fireside and gave them hot soup and bread from the oven. After the soup, warm and dry, they sat by the fire in silence. The gypsy woman was covered in a black shawl. Her fingers were heavy with gold rings. She sat so proudly, Mouse, so peacefully. Then, without warning, she took Ma's hand and searched her palm. She said in her country accent, 'I see a long life of happiness and prosperity, surrounded by well-being.' Ma was delighted, of course, and went to get a bag of my old clothes for the baby. The gypsy woman kept looking at me. The fire crackled and Wind blew. She leaned toward the fire, rubbing her hands together, and whispered to me, 'I see your name on the lips of many. Listen to the words in the wind. Your freedom lies in your dreams.' As she left she touched my hair. 'It's a kind woman you are, Claire O'Brien,' she said 'and this child of yours has an aura of gold around her, bless her.' And she went on her way."

"I wonder what the gypsy meant by aura of gold?" said Mouse.

"I don't know," Chesca said, "but I hope she's right about Ma."

Mouse lay on the comforter, and Chesca kept her head against the window and looked at the stars until the two of them drifted off to sleep.

Just before first light, Owl called out. Standing on a branch of the fir tree by the window, he tapped on the glass with his orange beak. Chesca woke and stared into his round yellow eyes. She started to open the window but he turned his head, ruffled his feathers, let out an unusual cry, and was gone.

"Did he say *read*?" Chesca said. It had happened so fast she wondered if it happened at all. Mouse sat up from under the cloak.

"Owl thinks I should read," Chesca said.

Mouse yawned and rubbed her eyes.

Careful not to wake Aunt Dena and her Da, if he was even home, Chesca crept down the stairs. She eased the door to the dining room open, keeping it from creaking. Bookshelves filled the back wall of the dining room, containing hundreds of books bound in leather, horse magazines, and farm almanacs. The old chandelier caught the light of the moon and reminded her of better nights: nights of dinner parties, with her parents' friends gathered around the table, with chatter and laughter like song; days when the chandelier had sparkled.

In the moonlight, Chesca took a worn red book from its dusty place. In gold lettering its title read, *Howth and Her History*. She sat on the floor with the book in her lap. Maybe history held the answer. Malley seemed to think so. Mouse jumped down from her shoulder and sat on her knee as Chesca read.

She read about the early Greeks who came to Howth before the deluge and how the plague wiped them out, and about the Vikings and their raids. She turned the gold edged pages and read about the Saxon and

Norman conquests. Then she landed on a page that made her heart skip a beat. There it was, the story of Grace O'Malley.

"Malley tells it better," she said, looking at the name of the author, a Mr. Hugh Doyle. "This man hasn't a patch on Malley."

"How did she save her land?" said Mouse. "Does it say?"

There was a drawing of Grace with her cloak around her and her long hair held back with a gemmed clip, just as Malley had described her, standing beside a choppy sea, tall and beautiful.

Beneath the picture, Ma had written, '*Never fear standing tall. Love will always conquer all.*'

Chesca remembered her mother wanting to tell her the story of Grace. A special story, she'd said, an important story.

"You know what I think, Mouse? I think it's not Da that's supposed to save the farm, it's Ma."

She and Mouse looked at each other.

"It's not," said Mouse. "It's you."

"Me?" said Chesca. "What can I do? I couldn't save a fly."

"Me neither," said Mouse, "but you can trick ride and back-flip and the horses would do anything for you."

"That won't save the farm."

She thought she heard the gate slamming. Wind was blowing; she couldn't make out the words Wind was saying, only the creak of the ceiling rafters and the rattle of the barn's tin roof.

"Remember what the gypsy said?" Mouse jumped off the book. "Something about gold, and Wind and living your dreams. Maybe the answer is in your dreams."

"The last dream I remember was crazy. I was spinning in a cupcake so fast I woke up on the floor."

Mouse shrugged.

She closed the book and clamped it under her arm. She picked Mouse up. A hint of light broke through a stormy horizon. Chesca crept back to bed and pulled the comforter around them. She kissed the tip of her pointer finger and planted it on Mouse's head. "Sweet dreams, Mouse."

"That's it," Mouse whispered urgently. "It's not your night dreams. It's your daydreams."

Chesca looked out the bedroom window to the cracked black sky and bright pins of starlight. Owl stood on the ledge and blinked, his big yellow eyes warm and wise.

"Well, now," Chesca said, grinning at Mouse. "My daydreams are a whole different story."

Chapter 17

hesca's daydreaming came to an abrupt halt the following morning.

"Get your tennis attire on, and get in the car," Dena said. "I have business to attend to."

"I'm not going anywhere," Chesca said.

"Get in the car or we'll be eating hen for dinner, local hen…very local,' she said and directed her stare out the window to the hens pecking away in the yard.

Chesca stood on the tennis court at Howth Castle feeling small, although she was tall for her age. She pulled down her white pleated tennis skirt, trying to cover more of her bare legs. In the clubroom, groups of kids were laughing and joking around while doing an art class, others were dancing ballet. Sure they were laughing at her awkwardness and reputation as being the mouse whisperer. She kept her eyes to the mountain. She was not born to be here, in this castle with its cold grey walls, and old heaving presence. She did not belong.

The sun was shining and she could make out the trees along Whispering Lane in the distance. Maybe she would see Malley and the other horses grazing in the lower fields.

Pablo, a sweet tennis instructor, stood on the other side of the net.

"Francesca," he said, "*por favor*, just tap the ball with the racket." He executed the simplest of serves. She watched the ball sail by her.

"Keep your eye on the ball now, *bella*," he said, serving another. Chesca tried to hit it and missed.

"Stupid tennis," she said and wondered what Pig was doing. And what was Rooster painting? Now, he could teach these kids a few things about art. Another ball came flying at her and she took a swipe with the racket and again she missed badly.

She looked back to the mountaintop. Patiently, Pablo served another ball and Chesca, distracted by a movement on the mountain, dropped the racket and caught the ball.

"What do you think this is, darling, the Wild West?" Pablo smiled. "You must hit the ball, *si*, with the racket." He held up the racket to show her. He reminded her of Star and her Spanish dancing and how much fun she was missing in the meadows. This time Pablo shot a ball at her, and she plucked it from the air with one hand. Pablo shook his head.

Maybe Malley had ideas about saving the farm? Maybe he was daydreaming too? They must dream big now. Another ball came flying at her and again she caught it and this time threw it back nearly hitting poor Pablo.

"I'm sorry," she said.

"I think, *bella* Frances-ca, you should be a catcher in, how-do-you-say, baseball." Pablo shook his head and smiled wearily.

"Pablo, would you mind if I took a break, I don't feel well," she excused herself.

In the bathroom, she sat, leaning against the bathroom wall, only the sound of the water filtering through the pipes and an occasional door shutting outside. She had a strong memory of a day with her mother.

The fog came rolling up from the lighthouse. The villagers would only see a veil around Howth Head. Chesca had felt as though she were in her own little world, protected by this soft gentle fog. Unlike nor'easters that came in the winter and beat on the East Mountain, bringing chaos and turbulent energy, the fog crept in quietly. Even the guillemots and gulls were silent. You never knew the rolling fog was coming, how long it would stay, or where it was going.

"Beware of the fox. He's smart and divisive," her mother told her. *Chesca was small, so her mother had knelt down and held her hand.*

"Once there was a fox, who waited for the fog to come in before he took one of the new lambs on the moor. Who would have known it was coming, the fog, so thick and concealing? But he did, and he used it to get

the lamb. The poor ewe did not even know her baby was gone until the fog lifted. So beware of the fox in the mist, Chesca."

She dropped her racket and walked out of the bathroom. Out the doors of the summer camp recreational room, all the way around to the front of the ancient castle, to the very place Grace had come to when she came to visit Howth. She stood at the huge oak doors with heavy cast iron hinges. While the door loomed large, black and uninviting, she thought about how Grace had been refused dinner, and how the refusal by the Earl had denied her existence as a chieftain, a queen, and a warrior.

A breeze gently blew as she turned from the door and saw the most beautiful sight, the most perfect view of the Mountain. She saw what Grace saw and understood why Grace had sent her bravest horse to protect it. Now it was her turn. No, it was not time to dream, it was time to put dreams into action.

That evening Da was home for his dinner, to shower, change his clothes and return to the hospital. He rarely left Ma's side now. Chesca was washing and peeling potatoes. She wanted to talk with him after dinner, alone, without Dena around. She was always around.

He walked into the kitchen, his hair still wet from his shower, his face unshaved, and his shirt wrinkled. He sat at the kitchen table; he looked lost in thought, gazing out the window.

"Da..." she dropped the potato peeler.

Aunt Dena marched into the kitchen with the bills she had been gathering from poor postman Pete. She laid them in front of him, as if showing him something he had never seen before. She tapped the big red letters with her painted and polished red fingernail.

"Tell me. What you are doing about these?"

"None of your business. Stay out of it." Her dad was upset but still not enough to give her that kick in the behind she deserved.

"Too late. I won't let my sister live like this anymore," Aunt Dena said, fixing a loose strand of hair.

"Let it be, Dena. Just let Claire be, for once."

"You might not be interested in her future, but I am!"

"DENA. Leave it. I don't even know if she has a future." Her dad was red in the face and Chesca didn't know what to do.

"That's the problem with you, Thomas, you give up. You don't fight for anything.

"Don't preach, Dena. Not now. I know what I'm doing."

"What is it exactly, that you are doing? You're losing your farm, your daughter is delusional and your wife is so tired she won't even wake up to come home to this mess. Why don't you just sell it?"

"No." Da jumped up from the table. "That's not what Claire wants."

"You still don't see what she wants Thomas. That's it. I've had enough," Dena said. "I came here to help you out. And still I get no thanks from either of you." She looked from Chesca to Da.

Da got up, pushed his chair back, stormed out of the kitchen and pounded upstairs. Aunt Dena was about to go too, leave for good. Go on back to Dublin. Chesca was sure. She wanted to scream at her, to go. She wanted to run and open the door for her and kick her on the way out. But she couldn't breathe. She just watched her, willing her out the door.

Aunt Dena picked up her bag and straightened her skirt and looked to the door, flustered, but something made her stop. They both looked out the window at the same time.

A man got out of a hunter-green Jaguar and began to battle the gate. He pulled the gate, pushed it, tried to lift it, and then kicked it.

Massive grey clouds shifted across the evening sky. The fire was burning low on the hearth and the kitchen was getting dark.

"That bloody gate," Aunt Dena said.

Dena kept her eyes on the man as he finally heaved it open. She smiled, as though she knew who he was. Chesca watched him as he got back into his car. Six foot, maybe taller; lean, clean-cut, wearing a well-pressed navy tweed suit.

"Bankers," said Chesca. "Do they ever leave you alone?" But the shiny car rolled into the yard.

"I love Jaguars," said Aunt Dena, watching his every move.

The man parked in front of the house. Aunt Dena checked her hair in the mirror and applied a new coat of lip-gloss. She walked into the hall and swung the front door open before the man even knocked. She smiled her smile.

"Are you the lady of the house?" the man said, and threw a cigar end onto the ground. He was carrying a briefcase. He offered Aunt Dena his hand and they shook without losing eye contact. She stepped back to let him in.

"Delighted to meet you," he said.

"I am the lady, for the moment. Although," she looked at his ring finger, "I can't speak too much of this house." She threw her disdain into every word.

"I'm honored. Ms. Flaherty, is it?" he said, with a thin lipped smile.

"Yes," Dena beamed.

"Is it Thomas O'Brien you're looking for?"

The man nodded. They appraised each other. She waved him toward the kitchen.

He nodded to Chesca and stood by the fire.

"Travers, Devlin Travers," he said to her.

Chesca felt that rising blush. What sort of a banker was he? She didn't know where to look and settled on the low flames behind him. Mr. Travers had steely blue eyes. He removed his black trilby hat, revealing a full head of silver hair. He reminded her of someone, but she could not think whom. The hairs on her arms were standing up. She rubbed them wanting to move towards the fire but he was there. Something about him made her very uncomfortable. He was watching her as if she had something he wanted. She looked at him sharply and he did not look away.

Aunt Dena was calling Da. Chesca stood awkwardly in the middle of the kitchen.

"Are you from the bank?' she said.

He rocked on his heels and put his hands in his suit pockets. "Not really the bank, more like an interest of the bank."

Da came in and they shook hands. Aunt Dena went about making a pot of tea. The two men sat down at the kitchen table and Chesca sat by the stove, watching.

"It's been a good summer so far, thank God," the man said. "Warm days."

"The hay is in," her dad didn't look too happy.

"Good, good," the man said.

"What can I do for you?" said Da.

"I represent an investment consortium called Gem Capital," Mr. Travers said.

Her Da's face was blank.

"On the word of a good friend, I'm here to make an enquiry about the possible sale of your property." The Travers man leaned over the table towards her dad as if they were the only people in the room, but Da leaned back in his chair.

Dena put the cups on the table, lingering by Mr. Travers' side.

"Thank you, Miss Flaherty," he said.

"It's Dena. Call me Dena." She straightened her hair and handed him a spoon. Da gave Dena a dark look. Mr. Travers kept his eye on him, as well he should. Da was not in a good humor.

"And what friend would that be, Mr. Travers?" he asked.

"I play golf with Mr. Davis. He suggested you might consider a better option than his."

"So," Da said. "Mr. Davis sent you to buy the farm from under us, at a cut rate. Is that it?" He got up and pushed in his chair. "Talk about kicking a dog when he's down. Did he also tell you it was a particularly convenient time, with my wife in the hospital?"

Mr. Travers drummed on the kitchen table with his soft fingers.

Chesca watched Aunt Dena. She stood by the fire and fanned herself with a magazine, her eyes never leaving the man. Chesca wanted to throw the milk jug at her.

"I'm so sorry to hear that," he said.

"The farm is not for sale."

There…her father had said it: Not for sale. Chesca let out a breath.

"I must have gotten the wrong information," Mr. Travers said, glancing at Aunt Dena.

"Thomas, think about it," she said.

That witch. There she was again, stirring the pot, causing trouble.

The cuckoo on the wall clock shot out, signaling five o'clock. Mr. Travers pulled up his cuff; a gold watch with a row of diamonds either side sparkled in the light.

"I believe the time is incorrect," he said.

"I believe," said her father, "the time is just right."

These were the words Chesca had waited all her life to hear her father say, but…it was not permission to ride Malley. She nearly smiled anyway. Her dad was showing him the door. *Go on Da. You tell him.*

"I think you should leave," he said. Chesca could see he was being polite.

Mr. Travers opened his oxblood leather briefcase. "Mr. O'Brien," he said, "I think you'll find the offered price is not at any cut rate."

He put a folded piece of paper on the table and placed a business card on top of it. "Call me if you reconsider." He put his hat on and tipped it to Aunt Dena. He stopped at the only remaining picture on the wall, the photograph of Malley in a full rear that Ma had taken last summer.

"That horse," he said, "he reminds me of one I saw in France in the most amazing show. A spectacular evening, very entertaining. A pleasant day to you."

He touched his hat, saluting Chesca in a gentlemanly fashion, and walked out the door.

"An amazing show," she whispered.

Wind rattled the window. Aunt Dena followed Mr. Travers to the door and waved him goodbye.

"What a charming man," she said.

Da picked up the piece of paper, looked at it, then crumpled it and threw it in the slops bucket. Without a word he went back upstairs.

Chesca sat by the fire, watching the flames flicker. *A show, an amazing show.* The words jumped around in her head like the flames in the fire. She closed her eyes.

"What are you smiling at?" Aunt Dena said. "Your father is being very unreasonable."

"He'll never sell," said Chesca.

"It's only a matter of time. I spoke to Mr. Davis."

"You did what?" Chesca said. She looked at her aunt; glared at her. Chesca wanted to scream.

Dena grabbed her handbag looking for a cigarette, rooting around searching for the pack. "Who do you think you are?" she said. "You should try to help your parents, like me. You selfish, selfish girl."

She took out a cigarette, and then, as if another person had slipped inside her body, she looked out the window, lit it, and smiled. "What a charming, handsome man, the kind of man who appreciates décor, class." She blew the stream of smoke in the air. As if remembering something, she shook her head and picked up the business card and read it, fanning herself with the little card and wearing her pert smirk.

"Weren't you on the way to Dublin?" Chesca said.

"Not so fast!" she said. "It seems my work is not finished here." Then she turned on her heels, walked to the compost bucket and picked out the piece of paper, read it, then let it drop.

"Well, well," she said. "Who'd have thought?"

Chapter 18

For days Chesca sat in her nook by the window and thought about a show. Sometimes she got excited, other times she dismissed her ideas and tried to push back the lingering fear of failure.

On the fourth day, Wind gusts kicked up over Ireland's Eye, and the white caps rolled and crashed. Chesca remembered one night her mother had sat on her bed and read to her about a show in France, with lights and music and horses.

"Mouse," she said, so suddenly she frightened Mouse awake. "We need the good-luck book."

Mouse dashed to help her and disappeared under the bed.

Chesca found it in the bookcase. "Here it is, Mouse."

Mouse popped her head out of a wicker basket. "The answers are always in a book," she said. "Sure, they're great things altogether."

Chesca took it and sat back in her nook. On the cover was an aerial photograph of a castle, surrounded by a huge moat and enclosing lush gardens, a racetrack, grandstand, and what looked like a second castle. She leafed through the pages and slowly took in every detail: the twinkling lights, the grand curtains at the entrance to the arena, and the show. *Les Plus Belles Ecuries du Monde*, she read. The Most Beautiful Stables in the World. Mouse jumped on to her shoulder to get a better view.

"Long ago, Mouse," Chesca said, "a man, a king, believed he would return from the dead, to live as a horse." She looked at Mouse. "So what else would a French king do but build a stable fit for a king?"

"Ooh, la, la," said Mouse.

Chesca laughed, "Exactly."

She turned a page and pointed to a palomino in a graceful stride. "Every month, for weddings, Christmas, or special occasions, they put on a show."

"Who does?" said Mouse.

"The family that owns the castle."

"Does it pay the bills?" said Mouse.

"I bet it does. Look at the beautiful costumes."

There were pictures of the insides of stables and of an arena with a sawdust-covered floor and thick stone walls and a domed ceiling, cathedral-like. There were people sitting on wooden benches all the way around. There were statues high on the walls of ancient gods and goddesses on their warhorses. In the middle of the arena was the black horse in an elegant canter. A spotlight shone on him, as if he were a star on Broadway.

"A show, Mouse, with music and lights and storytelling in a castle. I wonder if it was here, at Chantilly, France, where Mr. Travers saw the amazing stallion he spoke of."

"Smoky pants?" said Mouse. "He doesn't know the front end of a horse from the back."

Chesca turned the page. "Do you think Star would be able to do this?" she said. The picture showed a Lipizzaner horse performing a complicated Courbette. The white stallion flew through the air, all four hooves off the ground.

"Sure she will. Star loves all that jumping around and showing off," said Mouse.

"Maybe." Chesca put the book down and looked out the window.

"Where will we get a castle from?" said Mouse.

Chesca smiled. "Castle? No, Mouse, we have the Mountain!"

She picked up her pad. She wrote a scene of Star dancing, and her trick riding. She thought Pig could do a number but changed her mind. (Pig was unpredictable.) She would somersault and back flip off the horses, to music. They would do what they did best, only better. The Murphy sisters popped into her thoughts and the girls at school and all the girls that thought she was strange to want to ride a horse up-side-down. What would they think? Would they laugh at her? Would they even come? She hoped they did come, but not laugh, she hoped they cheered.

She wrote page after page, wrote and rewrote. She drew sketches and made lists. The fog crept in and rested like a cloud on Howth Head.

A bark drew her attention to the window. She opened it and peered out into the foggy orchards. Polly emerged from behind an apple tree.

"Malley wants to know when you're coming to the Brandy Banks. He's worried about you," she said.

"Soon. I'll come to the meadows tomorrow. I'll make an excuse. I'll say Star is sick."

"She is. She's bored sick."

"That'll do."

"I'll tell Malley," said Polly. She looked around, sniffing the air.

Chesca heard a car pull up in front of the house.

"Tell him, we have a show to do, a brilliant, dazzling mountain-saving show."

"About what?"

"About what we do best."

Polly panted and watched her, waiting for more information. The foghorn at the Bailey lighthouse bellowed a warning that rang around the mountaintop. "I better skedaddle," said Polly. She crept along the stone wall and bolted towards the meadows.

Chapter 19

There was a loud rapping on the front door. Owl hooted from the orchard. Chesca ran across the landing and looked out the window. Below her was the silver head of Mr. Travers, a cloud of cigar smoke around him. He was holding two brown paper bags of take-out from Howth Chipper, and there was a bottle tucked under his arm.

"Beware of the fox in the mist," whispered Chesca.

The smoke rose up into the fog until they were one. Chesca heard her Aunt Dena coming up the stairs and dashed back to her desk.

"Stay in your room," Aunt Dena said. "This is business. Do you hear me? And you better tell that flock of seagulls on the roof to take off. My friend is a hunting man."

Chesca heard the key turn in its lock. She ran at the door and kicked it. She could hear the click of heels descending the stairs.

"Believe me," said Mouse, "we're safer in here."

"I'm a prisoner in my own home. I tell you, when she's gone from the farm, that's when we'll be safe," Chesca said. She picked up her pen and got back to her show.

A murmur of chatter and laughter rose from the kitchen. The smell of spices and cigar smoke drifted up the stairs. The pop of a wine bottle brought on another round of laughter from a very happy Aunt Dena. Chesca could stand it no longer; she threw down her pen and pushed open her window.

"Real quiet now," she said to Mouse.

"No," said Mouse, with her look of panic.

"Be brave, Mouse."

Chesca put her in her pocket. Sitting on the window ledge, she swung her legs out. She knew every inch of the drainpipe. Quietly, she shimmied down, landing lightly on her feet. She tiptoed to the front of the house and sat underneath the open kitchen window. If there were seagulls on the roof, they were being very quiet.

"I knew the first time I laid eyes on you," cooed Mr. Travers, "that you would see the beauty of my proposal."

Dena laughed. "I'm sure I will, Devlin. I told Mr. Davis this place had potential."

"Beyond potential, it's perfect." He sounded charming and smooth. Chesca nearly liked him, but she remembered what foxes were like, cunning. "Mr. Davis said you're a very reasonable person."

"And I am," said Dena.

"Look what we have here: three hundred and fifty acres." Mr. Travers sounded like he had won the sweepstakes. "Mr. Davis, he knows what side his bread is buttered. He gave me the drawings of the East Mountain, three hundred and fifty wild acres, crying out for development."

"The dirty traitor," Chesca whispered.

"What's development?" said Mouse, but Chesca only shook her head. She dared a peek and watched them as he unrolled large prints. He held a model of a white painted fancy building and put it to one side, before sitting down to eat. Chesca ducked.

"I couldn't agree more," said Aunt Dena. "Level it."

Chesca froze. So that was her mantra. Level it. Oh my God, she meant their home.

"It's not as big as my last project, a shopping center on the ancient grounds of Kildare, but this place has the potential to go a long way.

Mouse shivered.

"Could you pass the salt? Thank you Dena, you are kind."

"Think nothing of it," she said.

There was a clink of silverware.

"As I was saying, I have put together, with the power of the top legal and investing minds in Dublin, a proposal for the sale of the East Mountain, and they agree, its time has come. The last undeveloped coastline in County Dublin is ready for the big-time."

"What?" squeaked Mouse.

"Shush," said Chesca.

"I'm sure I can help you," said Dena. "Do we have similar ideas, mansions around a golf course?"

"We can definitely work together, but golf?" Mr. Travers laughed a deep hearty laugh. "I'm sure you can think bigger than that, Dena Flaherty."

"How big?" said Dena.

"Think hotel. Think casino. Think cruise port. Think mega-mansions, Dena. Think big, really big."

The pop of a champagne cork startled Chesca.

"I can see it, Devlin, I can see it," said Dena, to the clink of glass on glass.

"Wonderful, Dena Flaherty," he said.

"Remind me, what does Mrs. Travers think of it all?"

"Oh Dena, no, there is no Mrs. Travers."

"Well, then," said Dena. "Here's to a new, exciting partnership."

"Upwards and onwards," he said. They touched glasses once more and laughed way too long.

"They want to put an end to the mountain herself," Chesca whispered. "Da will never agree. Ma will never sell to them. Never."

"Never," said Mouse and passed out, flat on her back in the corner of the pocket.

"Oh, Mouse." Chesca picked her up and put her on her knee.

"I've been making ground with Thomas," said Dena. "I had a few of those little chats that you suggested. You're right, he's coming around; seems more resigned."

"The man knows his time is up," said Mr. Travers.

"For my sister's sake," Dena said. "The idea of the girl in a quiet home in the country is comforting to Thomas."

"As indeed it should be," said Mr. Travers. "I mean the burden of this place. He should be happy to have an offer."

"Just the other day," said Dena, "a rooster, a turkey, and a pig were seen roaming the village, unattended, outside the art gallery standing on their hind legs looking in the window. Sure they're wild, I tell you, wild, this place is a madhouse. Level it."

"Scandalous. Level it indeed."

A seagull began to screech, but they paid no attention to it.

"But this is the thing," Aunt Dena said. "I'm not sure *who* he'll sell it to. He may not like the idea of a casino."

There was a chorus of screeches from the roof.

Aggh, aghh aghh, the gulls were beginning to spread the word. *Dirty traitors…*

"You leave Thomas to me, dear woman. He just needs a man-to-man. All you have to do is keep guiding him in the right direction, and the kid, too. I have an idea, a Plan B that Thomas O'Brien will love."

"Tell me more," Aunt Dena said, sounding all happy and cozy.

Chesca grabbed a flowerpot to hurl at her. PLAN B, Mouse was up, standing on Chesca's knee jumping around in a little dance of panic. The birds were getting louder. *Lying, dirty traitors…*

"No," Mouse said.

Chesca looked at the pot and put it down.

"What's a casino?" said Mouse, the tears welling up again.

Aggh, aghh, there was a heavy flapping noise, wings beating in the air.

"You don't want to know." Chesca had heard enough. "We're going to the Brandy Banks."

"What's all the commotion about?" Mr. Travers said, coming toward the window.

Owl hooted, and took off into the night. Chesca put Mouse back in her pocket and ran as if the devil were at her back. The gate swung open, the seagulls dived from the roof and flew around her, hiding her as she ran into Whispering Lane.

Chapter 20

Shssh, steady now, child, whispered Lane. The tops of the elms swayed like drunken sailors. The foghorn belted out one more bellow from the lighthouse. Chesca ran down the dark Lane, holding Mouse to her chest. Wind came gusting down from the trees.

Time is of the essence, said Wind.

"Can you believe it?" she said.

I've been around a long time, said Lane. *I can believe anything.*

The fog rolled away from her. A half-moon hung in a cloudless ink-black sky.

Mouse was quiet in her pocket. Chesca looked around for her friends. The circle was empty and there was no movement around the cottage. The fog was on its way across the moors, rolling north.

"Malley?"

"Are we ready to begin?" said Malley, emerging from the darkness. His velvety nostrils were opened wide, and in the silence he snorted a hot breath and shook his head.

"Oh, Malley, do we have a job to do," Chesca said.

In the distance, in the shadow of the Mountain, the screech of a vixen pierced the night and she knew people would toss in their beds and wonder if it was the Banshee and her call of death, and would she come to take them?

"You won't believe what they're planning," she said, "I can't believe she'd trick her own sister." Chesca's hand trembled and tears welled in her eyes.

"Take it easy," said Malley.

Star galloped towards her. Maureen and the girls turned away from the cliff side out of the fog and came to the circle. The others followed, trotting, cantering, eyes forward, looking to her.

"They need you now," Malley whispered.

"Aunt Dena and a Mr. Travers…" Chesca said.

"The scheming low-life. Scoundrels of the highest order," Pig was taking a big breath to continue his insults.

Owl hooted from the oak tree. Malley winked at Owl and touched Chesca's elbow with his nose.

"We know all about them," he said. "Forget about them for now."

"Forget them? But it's time to do something. Something big," Chesca said, stretching her arms in either direction to show them all, she meant really big.

Little steps, child, blew Wind.

Chesca scrunched her hands into a ball and looked to the night sky. "Am I the only one who understands that this could be the end of us all?"

"Every leader needs a plan," Malley said.

"Yes! Yes, but they have plans. They have very, very, big hideous plans."

The circle was getting tighter. The old horses had joined them, and Chesca could feel the warmth of the cows, and smell the sweet grass.

Little steps, whispered Wind.

"Remember Grace," said Malley.

"Grace?" said Chesca. "Was she born a brilliant warrior, a brave leader?"

Malley shifted his gaze from the ocean to her. "Chesca, sure Grace was not born anything except a feisty little baby."

"What was she doing before she went to England?"

Malley seemed to hesitate, looking out towards the sea, always looking to sea when he thought of Grace, as if she was out there like some believed she was. They believed she was sailing still.

"She was on the gallows, with a rope around her neck. Accused of treason and piracy against the Crown."

There was a collective gasp. Star, especially, was appalled. Turkey flapped his wings in the oak tree.

"But she survived." Chesca watched Malley. He turned sharply and stared at her.

"YES. As we'll survive," he said.

"Right, Malley. So here's our plan," she said. "Listen friends, everyone...we are putting on the show of all shows." The hens blinked and then clucked and the cows lowed. "We are going to do the show of Grace and Malley. Here in the circle," she said, walking around it, "we will have a bonfire, and music and lots of Grace O'Malley action, and an auction for all our fabulous farm products."

"I could paint the backdrop for each scene," said Rooster.

"I could conduct the songs," said Turkey.

"That's the spirit," Chesca smiled. "I've seen Grace in a book, and Ma's words about her: 'Never fear standing tall, love will always conquer all.'"

Wind chuckled.

"What are you laughing at?" said Chesca. "We'll need help, for sure. Someone who knows a thing or two about shows."

Polly sniffed the air. Her ears pricked. They all stood in silence. There was movement in the trees and the crack of a branch, and a beam of white light shone among the tree trunks.

Malley reacted first. He arched his neck, stamped his hoof rapidly once, twice, then again. He snorted. His eyes searched the shadows

"Is that you, Chesca?" came a deep voice. The beam of a flashlight bobbed and swung, and out of the darkness came a large figure in a long black raincoat.

Chapter 21

amper?"

"Aye," Bamper said.

Chesca let her breath out. The cows gave a soft sigh.

"I was out walking," said Bamper. "Checking the fences. You could do with a bit more light, what with the fog and all." He looked toward the mountaintop. The moonlight shone on his weathered face. "You never know, it may turn back around. It's funny like that, the fog."

He bent and placed the flashlight next to Chesca. Its beam shone towards the circle. Malley relaxed and sniffed at the flashlight and Chesca patted his nose.

"I'm fine, Bamper. I was just out for a little walk, myself."

"Well," he said, with his habitual blink. "Good, then I'll be on my way."

"Bamper? What do you think about a show, here on the mountain? With horses, lights, dancing and pirates?"

"Pirates. Sure I love the pirates. Who doesn't?"

Chesca smiled.

"What would your intentions be with a show, kiddo?" said Bamper.

"I intend," said Chesca, "to bring Grace O' Malley back to life and save the mountain."

"Do you, now? Big task, but no better girl. I could help you out with the sound and whatnot."

Malley nudged her.

"Maybe, Bamper, you could help me rig a little stage, right over there."

"That would make a great stage," Bamper said. "I could rig the lighting and sound from the cottage. Run it all off the tractor. Our backstage could be under the oak tree."

The Kerry Cows had moved off to retire along the hedge, and the ponies and yearlings were asleep, standing like statues scattered about the meadows. A young wandering hedgehog sat up and looked around. Pig grunted. The hedgehog curled into a ball and rolled away into the darkness, and they both watched her go.

"A few lengths of wood from the shed could get you some benches," Bamper said. "We can't have the old ones from the village sitting on the ground." He gave a small chuckle, as if to himself. "I'll get to work on that in the first light," he said.

"Spare nothing," said Chesca. "If you need wood for the stage, strip the barn."

Malley looked at her. Owl screeched.

"What have we got to lose?" said Chesca,

With a tip of his cap, Bamper said in old Irish, "Oiche amhait. Good night, Chesca." And he started back the way he came.

"Night, Bamper," she said.

Star watched him, then turned and gave Chesca a stern look.

"Wait, Bamper. Do you know anyone who can make costumes?"

"I do," said Bamper over his shoulder. "Maro Malone, the musician's wife. Didn't she make all the costumes for the Christmas play? They were the talk of Dublin."

Chesca could hardly see him now, but she heard his deep voice, his pleasant lilt in the dark as he moved into the shadows. He never did say much, but when he did, Chesca felt his words wrap around her like a pair of strong, comforting arms. She wondered if anyone else felt like that. She smiled. He was shy, but maybe, with a bit of coaxing, he could be the narrator for the show.

"I'll ask Maro," he said. "And sure, maybe Peter Malone might play a tune for us?"

"Thanks, Bamper," said Chesca. "Because Bamper, they want to build a casino. A Mr. Travers and Aunt Dena, they want to build a hotel, too."

It was quiet and Chesca thought Bamper was gone. Then he spoke from the shadows:

"I think Sunday morning Mass would be a great place to start recruiting foot soldiers. Make me a list of what you need, and at Mass just give me the nod. I'll take care of the rest."

Chapter 22

Sunday morning started off badly and didn't improve. Chesca and Turkey sat on the garden wall. She heard the clatter of hooves and made out the distinct outline of Mary Murphy, her sister Aileen and Maggie Smith from the farm at the Bailey trotting toward the barn gate. She thought they would ride by their barn and go to gallop on the cliff path, but they turned and trotted into the farmyard, towards them. Turkey began to spread his wings.

"They must have heard about your mother," he said as they approached.

"They can get off our mountain," Chesca said and clenched her fists.

"Let them talk," Turkey gobbled and hopped up into a tree.

They pulled their ponies to a halt. It was Mary who had the news. But instead of the smug look of I-who-knows-everything-and-you-who-are-mad look, her face held some other kind of knowledge. Maggie Smith sat on her new jumping pony that was highly-strung and a little skittish, prancing on the spot.

"Chesca, my father said your Da is selling the land. Is it true?" said Mary.

"Get off my mountain, he is in his..."

"It's just what he heard," said Aileen, her big thick braid hanging over her shoulder. Her glasses had splashes of mud on them. "We hope it's not true."

What did they want? They have been ignoring her for years. Now they came with lies.

"My father would never sell, not in a million years."

"Mr. Davis is helping the sale, and I hear, your aunt is, too. If I were you Ches, I'd try and stop them. Where would the horses go?" Maggie said meekly. She used her nickname. Chesca thought for one split second that Maggie cared, but Mary sat there watching her.

158

"Nowhere. They are going nowhere. Now get off my land," she said. She caught the eye of Mary and Mary opened her mouth to say something else but shut it and turned and kicked her pony into a trot. It was Maggie who said, "I hope your Mom is feeling better." But Chesca didn't hear her. She was already in a handstand and stayed that way until she knew they were gone. She thought a million different thoughts in a very short time.

"He'd never sell. They are just being cruel," she said. There was the scrape of the kitchen window lifting and the morning air was spoiled.

"Time for Mass, Frances-ca," Aunt Dena shouted out the kitchen window.

Chesca fell in a heap. Wind blew the window shut with a bang, nearly crowning Aunt Dena.

Chesca stood up, red in the face, ready to tell her to get lost; go, for once and for all, but Mouse tapped her on her shoulder with her tail.

"Malley said not to take any notice of her," she said, "until the show is over."

Chesca kicked a stone. Wind blew, pushing her toward the house.

Go, Wind said.

"It's not you that has to wear that stupid Sunday dress." Chesca shook her head and went up to her room and put the dress on and stood in front of the mirror. The satin skirt billowed out like a cream puff with blue ribbons and bows. She wore white socks and new white shoes. Her hair was curled.

"I look like a clown," she said.

"It's not for long," Mouse said.

Chapter 23

Howth Church, with its grey stone steeple, the tallest building in the village, stood peering over the shops and restaurants. The only other building of its stature was the castle, less than a mile away.

Chesca stood in the fifth pew near the aisle. Aunt Dena stood solemnly beside her, hands together in prayer. Her Sunday hat was a cream pillbox with the tip of a peacock feather pinned to one side. The church was filling up fast. Father Dunwoody came out of the vestibule. He looked at Aunt Dena and gave her the slightest smile. He welcomed everyone and began the Mass. Chesca glanced around for her father. Beside her were the empty spaces, the seats where her mother and father sat every Sunday.

Bamper stood across the aisle. Chesca could see him out of the corner of her eye. Inside his prayer book was the list she had given him of the people they would need: a director, actors, musicians, a singer, a dancer, a printer, an auctioneer. He had squinted at the list, blinked his blink, and put it in his pocket.

Mrs. Dillon from the flower shop had walked past Chesca, not recognizing her, which suited Chesca. The church was undergoing a renovation, and the old pews on the left side had been replaced with modern, less ornate, ones. She wondered where the old pews were. They could come in handy. Suddenly everything around her was relevant to the show and saving the farm and her mother. The early morning light shone through the stained-glass window, and dust motes danced in its rays.

"In the name of the Father and of the Son," said the congregation. Aunt Dena made the sign of the cross. She was looking radiant. Then Chesca understood why: she saw the silver head of Mr. Travers in the front pew. He held his trilby in one hand and blessed himself with the other. Aunt Dena watched his every move. He turned and nodded to her. She gave him a flirtatious smile and stood a little straighter.

Chesca turned her gaze to the cross behind the altar and listened as Father Dunwoody spoke to the people of Howth. She watched the dust motes spin in the light. An old woman coughed. A child protested having to be silent. Chesca waited.

Father Dunwoody began to hand out communion. The congregation formed a line. A tapping came from the balcony and the conductor began waving his arm. He had a very long chin and his hooded eyes looked out over a pair of spectacles. The organist pressed a long low note. The choir began to sing.

Now the green blade riseth from the buried grain.

Everyone joined in.

Mrs. Dillon knelt and received the Host. Chesca bowed her head. Bamper saw her and wrote *General Manager—Mrs. Dillon.* Next came Captain Covey of the *Asgard.* Chesca nodded; Bamper wrote.

Mr. and Mrs. Nesbit from the bakery, gossips of the highest order, were next up, and Chesca remained still, remembering her mother's words on gossips. They do no good.

Old Jimmy Hickey and Cod Nickels, a young fisherman, were next. Chesca thought for a second. Bamper watched, and she nodded. Bamper smiled and wrote their names beside *Pirates*.

Aunt Dena glared at her. "Stay still," she hissed. Chesca faced the altar and did not move.

"Body of Christ," said Father Dunwoody.

"Amen," said Mrs. Murphy. Chesca coughed. Bamper wrote.

Aileen and Mary Murphy walked by her to receive. Chesca knelt, put her head down to hide her face. The last thing she needed was the Murphy girls to see her now.

At the end of communion the choir sat down. The conductor again tapped his podium. Tighie Connell, a pale and frightened-looking teenage boy, cleared his throat and stood up and looked out from under his long hair with eyes like a fawn's. He began to sing, and it was the sweet voice of an angel that rose into the air. He reached for notes so high Chesca thought the glass would crack. Everybody held their breath as his mouth shaped the last notes of the *Ave Maria.* It was so beautiful it brought a tear to Bamper's tough Dublin eye. Chesca nodded twice. Bamper wrote and closed his book.

"To conclude," said Father Dunwoody, looking up from his Bible, "I would ask everyone"—he snapped the Bible shut—"to say a prayer for Claire O'Brien, who, as you all know, is in the hospital."

Chesca's heart stopped.

"For her family..." The priest held his hands out, Christ-like, toward Chesca. She felt her face turn red. Every head in the church turned to look at her. She heard the murmur, "*Is that Ches? Ah, bless her heart. The poor, poor, child.*"

"...For her wonderful aunt, for taking such great care of her." Father Dunwoody closed his eyes in quiet admiration. "For Thomas O'Brien, as he struggles to see the way ahead. We know that the decisions he makes, in these dark days, will be the best for his family." He pressed his thin lips together and tried to give a reassuring smile.

'It's true," whispered Mr. Dillon. "Thomas must be selling the farm."

Mrs. Dillon scowled at him. "I don't believe it."

But Chesca had heard him.

Mr. Travers turned and winked at Aunt Dena. Chesca could feel the eyes of the village on her. Her aunt, standing over her as she knelt, placed a hand on her head. It was too much. She shook the hand off and growled at her aunt. There was an awkward silence as everyone looked at her. Why in the name of God did she think anyone would help her?

"The poor child, what have they done to her? The get-up of her," said Mrs. Dillon, throwing Dena an icy glare.

Dena smiled. She signaled the priest to continue.

"Go in peace," said Father Dunwoody.

Chapter 24

hesca bolted out the church door and ran toward the meadows wishing her mother would appear before her at every turn. She ran through puddles and jumped ditches. She stumbled on the rocky road, fell and scraped her knees. She took the abandoned tram tracks, jumped over a fence and, blinded by tears, she ran through thickets of wild gorse. She cursed her Aunt and prayed the spiders pinched her head all night while she slept, that the mice would pluck holes in her suits, that the birds would pick her up and take her back to Dublin, gone forever.

"Eleven year olds aren't supposed to save mountains," she shouted into the crashing waves under the cove.

When Chesca returned to the comfort of the barn, and the sweet smell of the new hay, she climbed the ladder to the loft and collapsed against a bale.

"I never knew you could run so fast," said Mouse, swinging on a ribbon of the dress to the hay bale.

"Mouse!" said Chesca. "Have you been with me all this time?"

"I get scared in the room without you," said Mouse.

"But you must stay in the jar when I'm with her." Chesca picked her up. "Mouse," she said, "we need to start rehearsals."

"Won't she come looking for you?" said Mouse.

"She doesn't give a hoot about me," said Chesca, leaning over the railing to look below. Bamper had used the wood from the stalls, dividing walls, and office. All the planking was gone, a stage and seating now in the Brandy Banks.

The barns doors swung open and Chesca ducked. Mr. Travers came in, followed by Aunt Dena. They stopped by the feeding bins. Chesca peeped down at them. Mr. Travers had his briefcase.

"There's something missing," said Aunt Dena.

"The child," said Mr. Travers.

"No, I mean in here. Something's gone."

"It'll all be gone soon. But what about the girl?"

"Such a contrary one," Aunt Dena said.

"She'll be back soon enough," laughed Mr. Travers. "When she gets hungry."

"But did she have to give me trouble now?"

"From what I hear at the club, it's the stallion that causes all the trouble," said Mr. Travers.

"Yes, they talk about this horse a lot, like some ferocious god. Absolutely no bother to me, I make sure the creatures come nowhere near the house. You must keep a strict hand in these matters."

Aunt Dena loosened Mr. Travers' necktie.

"There'll be no trouble," he said, "when he's in a meat can." He raised his chin, looked around the barn. "No more wild horses, no more pesky mice, no more difficult children."

Aunt Dena ran a hand over his shoulder and let it rest on his arm.

Chesca and Mouse looked at each other.

"Meat can?" Mouse squeaked.

There was a thud below. Mr. Travers had placed one of Chesca's heart-shaped rocks on one end of a roll of blueprints. He unfurled them over the feeding bins and picked up another rock and placed it with another thud. He pulled the *Joy* sign from Pig's trough and placed it in the middle of the blueprints.

"This," he said tossing his hand toward the loft, "would be the epicenter, so to speak."

Chesca and Mouse ducked.

"Housing the casino and hotel," he said, and gazed out the doors to the Irish Sea. "What do you say to the penthouse suite? Nice views, Dena my lovely."

"I'd say it has possibilities," said Aunt Dena.

"Possibilities indeed. And these," he said, pulling out a second set of papers, "these," he tapped them and Chesca and Mouse peeked over again as he swept his hand over the large blueprints, "are what Thomas fell for. He believes these plans will *save his farm!* See Dena? I told you everyone would win."

"You're genius, Devlin. Truly a win-win. Finally, my sister can have some peace."

"It's nearly time," Mr. Travers said. "Just keep your cool and gently guide him to sign." He lit a cigar. A cloud of smoke rose up to the roof.

"Keeping my cool," said Aunt Dena, "is what I do best."

The Jeep was pulling up to the house, and Mr. Travers rolled up the blueprints and put them back in his briefcase. He and Aunt Dena walked out and slammed the barn doors and bolted them. Chesca scrambled to the wall and peered through a crack. She could see Mr. Travers holding the door open as Aunt Dena got into the Jeep. Da was behind the wheel. Mr. Travers followed Aunt Dena into the back seat. Da, his face grey and tired, turned and shook hands with Mr. Travers, then he revved the Jeep and drove out of the yard towards the mountain and meadows.

Chesca pounded on the loft doors. The Jeep rattled in the distance. She kicked the doors, and they swung open. She grabbed the winch rope and swung down. Wind got behind her and pushed.

*Hurry, Chesca...*Wind said.

She landed and took off at a run. The gate rattled and banged. Star came galloping towards her, blowing hard. Chesca vaulted onto her back.

"They're con artists, blaggards, rogues..."

"Them, artists?" Star said.

"They're tricksters, not in a good way, Star."

Star sprang forward and galloped after the Jeep as fast as she could.

Chapter 25

Dad stood overlooking the Brandy Banks pointing to the stone walls and nodding slowly. The shysters stood nodding with him, with the Travers man puffed up like a prize pigeon. Chesca galloped towards them at a deadly speed.

"What on earth…?" Da said turning as Star came to a sliding halt in front of them.

"Don't listen to these two," she shouted. "Don't listen to a word they say. They're up to no good."

"I was going to talk to you tonight," Da said. He held his hand out for her to get off Star, but Chesca pulled back and stayed on Star, safe.

"Do you know what they plan on doing to the farm, to the animals?" she cried. Star began to shake her head and mane and step sideways.

"Chesca, it will be beautiful," he said. "The place will be all the better for the improvements. Think, there will be a home for everyone, here and in the country, and Bamper will keep his job. They have wonderful plans for the land."

"Lies! Tricks! They want to destroy the farm. They have two sets..."

Aunt Dena raised her eyes toward Heaven. "Such disrespect," she cut in quickly.

Her dad looked at her in that quizzical way he sometimes did, his brow deep with furrows.

"Chesca, it will make a beautiful *stud farm*. You can visit Malley any time you want," he said.

"Stud farm!" she said, brushing tears away. Star pranced, working up lather. "Da, they don't have plans for a stud farm, they want to build a bloody great big cruise ship, right over there," she pointed to the cove beside the Nose of Howth, "and a hotel, and a casino."

Mr. Travers drew on his cigar. Aunt Dena smiled.

"Frances-ca," she said. "Where ever did you get that silly idea?"

"I heard you."

"But darling Frances-ca, we know—in fact everyone knows—that you hear lots of things. Did you hear it perhaps, from one of the animals?" she laughed. "Really, Thomas, she does have a spectacular imagination. No wonder she has no friends."

"Mr. Travers has the plans right here," her dad said. "I've seen them. It will be the most beautiful stud farm."

"Yes, it will," said Mr. Travers, and released a puff of smoke.

"Da, you must believe me," Chesca said in a tearful whisper. "Da."

"Now Chesca, come on," he said. "Everyone knows you could never build a cruise port in the cove or the harbor."

Dena and Mr. Travers looked at each other, then back to her dad.

"Why?" said Aunt Dena.

"It's too shallow," he said. "Now go on back to the house, Chesca, and get out of those torn clothes."

"Don't sign," she said. "Please Da, don't."

"I have no choice." He was getting angry. She could see the blood reddening his cheeks. Mr. Travers was rolling out the stud farm plans on the bonnet of the car, and a contract.

A piercing whinny cut the air. Malley.

"I want to put on a show," Chesca said.

"What?" her dad was confused and agitated.

"What?" said Aunt Dena.

"I want to perform a show. With Star, and maybe music and lights."

"Now?" he said.

"In a few months. Just say yes."

"We leave at the end of the summer," he was looking out to sea. "Then we hand over the keys. That's the last word."

"Ma won't like this, not one little bit," Chesca said.

He turned away from her. He picked up the pen.

"Is she coming home?" said Chesca.

"Go," he said, his head down, looking at the contract.

"Is she?" Chesca shouted.

"I don't know. Nobody knows."

"I'm going to see her."

Was her dad crying too?

"How wonderful," said Aunt Dena. "A farewell show. It sounds delightful, Frances-ca."

"You liar. You absolute liar," she screamed at Dena.

Dena shook her head, slowly and turned to Da.

"She's been under a lot of stress. Poor Frances-ca."

Chesca turned and Star bolted, kicking divots of moss and clay that rose up in the air and rained down behind her.

Chapter 26

Angry clouds were moving across the sea toward the Brandy Banks. Chesca's torn dress flapped around her legs as Star galloped to the Banks. They ripped through the ferns and heather, popped a gully and jumped the stone wall. *We have to rehearse*, pleaded Chesca, and the clouds seemed to hesitate, turn, and move back out to sea.

"He's going to sign," shouted Mouse from her pocket.

"He doesn't know what he's doing," Chesca said. She shook her head, pulling her ponytail free.

Malley was waiting for her by the cottage. Donkey stood beside him, looking very anxious.

"We only have 'til the end of summer," Chesca said, and jumped down off Star.

The hens squawked and ran to pass the word around the mountaintop, up to where the wild goats roamed. Pig trotted out of the woods, his snout black from rooting in the dirt. The Kerry cows arrived.

"Da's going to sign," said Mouse waving her little paw frantically.

"We're still doing the show," Chesca said.

"What's the point?" Pig said. "We should have run them off the mountain when we had the chance. Now, we should run off the mountain while we still have a chance...Oh, My, God."

"Never fear," Chesca said, closing her eyes, "standing tall." She smelled the salt air. "Love will always conquer all." She opened her eyes. "Ma knows what she's talking about, even if Da doesn't. I can't believe he fell for all those lies. Everyone, Grace will help us. We must win by doing what we do best, we have no choice now."

They stood around the circle, watching her. The rain was in the distance now and the sun was breaking through the clouds. The old horses hobbled down from the hillside. The colts and fillies stood back and watched from the long grass and ferns as Chesca told them all, what they must do. All the while Malley stood behind her, watching her every move.

"I have a cloak, a very special cloak. I think it was Ma's. It's the most beautiful green velvet, with gems of red and emeralds. It has gold thread embroidery on the sides. It's exquisite!"

"Grace is here," Malley said and a deep silence came upon them. "Grace is here and will guide us," and they believed him.

"And what better story to tell." Chesca said. "We must bring her alive."

Chapter 27

alley called to Chesca and they walked down the bridle trail to the beach. The last rays of gold shone down on Howth Head. Herring gulls and kittiwakes were calling out around the ledges, seeking out their young before they slept. Three gulls hung in the sky like puppets on strings.

"What are you thinking about?" Chesca said.

"I'm thinking we can't rely on luck alone."

"We'll need help," she said. But that familiar feeling that people didn't like her because she was different crept over her.

Malley came to the water's edge, where the tide rippled backwards, retreating back into itself, chattering over pebbles. Chesca jogged to catch up with him, her boots crunching over scallop shells and periwinkles. They stood on the shore looking across at the village, not a football field away. The lights of the shops and restaurants were glowing in the dusk. The treetops lining the harbor road swayed in the wind.

"Maybe you can recruit some friends to help?" Malley said.

"All my friends are helping." Chesca looked at him and raised her brows. He knew that already.

"Maybe the girls from the other barns?"

"They will only torment us. Come on Malley, you know how they call us the funny farm."

"I'm not sure I do. I have never heard that," Malley said. He didn't look at her, as if it was not that important, and now that she thought about it, she couldn't remember when she heard them say it or even who said it. She felt a rising anger again at the thought of them saying it. Malley pushed her with his nose and she smiled at his playful gesture.

"Chesca," he said, "do you know what your name means and why your mother called you that?"

She remembered Ma telling her.

"When your mother called you, to be free," he said, "she meant, free forever."

"Free from the fox," she said.

"That's the plan," he said. "All of us, free from the fox, forever. Our task here is not just to save the farm but also to protect the Mountain against the fox, the developers and destroyers of all that is natural, forever. Do you see the difference? It's a monumental task, but we can do it."

From the tavern the notes of a flute cried out like a bird, and a fiddle mimicked Wind, whistling and wailing. Wind carried the music to their ears.

"Is that the kind of music we need for the show?" asked Malley.

Chesca smiled. "Yes. The tavern music hasn't changed much in the last few hundred years and it's exactly what we need. We should begin tomorrow."

"At dawn," Malley said.

"What night should we hold the show?"

"On the last full moon of summer," said Malley.

They walked back up the trail to the brook and looked back at the village, out past the ruby and amber lights of Dublin City, into the darkness.

"But Malley, before we do anything, there's something I must do," Chesca said.

"What's that?"

"I have to go see Ma."

Chapter 28

That's the one, dearie," whispered Nurse Veronica. "Go on, but be quick, love. I'll be"—she ran a finger across her throat—"if you're caught at this hour."

The moon over Dublin City shone in through the high narrow window at the end of the corridor, casting shadows on the peeling walls. Chesca found room 312 and looked back. Nurse Veronica was at her desk drinking a cup of tea. She nodded, and Chesca opened the door to Ma's room.

The room was quite dark. A table lamp glowed wanly. Ma lay asleep. Chesca could just make out her face.

"Ma?"

She looked peaceful; her skin pale, tired but beautiful. There were bandages around her head. Chesca touched her cheek.

"They cut your beautiful hair," she whispered.

She took her mother's hand. "Da's going to sell the farm," she said. "They're fooling him, Ma, but he won't believe me. There is nothing I can do to stop him. And Aunt Dena...." A heart monitor beeped. Chesca watched the green line peak and dive.

"I found the book about Grace O'Malley," she said, "and in it you wrote the words, 'Never let them take the land.' Were they her words Ma?"

She watched her lips for movement.

"I thought if we put on a show about Grace, with eight acts, eight small scenes of Grace's life set to music, with trick riding and Malley...well Malley being Malley, just showing everyone the Magic of Howth, we would win. We could pay the taxes and tell Mr. Travers that it was just a big horrible mistake and that the farm is not for sale. The farm would become a theater, with a full house every weekend. Wouldn't that do it, Ma?"

The machine beeped. Chesca held her mother's hand between hers.

"Star is dancing new steps all the time. She dances at night by the light of the moon. Even the old horses want to march in the show. They're excited, Ma." There was an empty silence. "We have a big job to do, then all will be well again. It'll be grand. It'll be better than grand."

Chesca bent, closed her eyes and inhaled the sweet smell of her mother's floral-scented nightdress. There was a squeak of rubber shoes in the hall, and Nurse Veronica stuck her head around the door.

"Can she hear me, Nurse Vee?" She kept her eyes on her mother, waiting for her to wake.

"Sweetheart," Nurse Veronica said, "it's time to get going. The late shift is nearly over. You can't be seen here."

"Can she hear me?"

Nurse Vee looked at her sadly. "Every word."

Chesca bent down.

"I'm going to get you some of Maureen's milkshake. It's pure magic." She kissed her on the cheek. "And don't you worry about me. I think that cloak is very special. I can feel it protecting me."

She gave Nurse Veronica a warm hug and hurried down the stairs and out of the hospital.

"Hurry, Chesca," Polly barked. She had been waiting by the door. Mouse poked up from inside Polly's shaggy coat. Chesca held her palm out. Mouse sprang onto her hand, then into her pocket. Chesca followed Polly across the lighted car park. She nearly missed the muddy old Jeep, but the green scarf caught her eye.

Her dad was in the driver's seat with his cap over his eyes, asleep. The scarf lay over his shoulder. Chesca moved to open the door and wake him, and then stopped. He looked out of place here, out of his farm, but there was nothing she could say now. If he didn't believe her about their lies, what could she say now to change his mind?

She ran out of the parking lot, crossed a green and climbed an embankment to the train tracks. She caught her breath and followed the iron threads of the track out of Dublin City.

In the light of the moon, Mouse peeked out of her pocket. Wind played a song in the trees, and Mouse hummed along. Chesca kept her eyes on the dark rise of Howth Head. As she marched the six miles back to her home on the Mountainside, the moon hung like an inviting new world, before her.

Chapter 29

She stood on Star's back, staring out at the cliffs and the Wicklow Mountain. She wore her cloak and held her hands to the side and on the count of three she tried for a back flip and nailed it, landing lightly on her feet, without Wind helping her.

Bamper said he would get what she needed on the list, but after Mass she doubted anyone would help her, which made her more determined to go it alone: just Bamper, steadily building the stage and getting the cottage fixed up. He had cleared away the gorse on the banks for seating and ran electrical wires from the stage to the cottage. He was a trouper. Then she counted to three and flipped again.

It was on a Friday morning that Bamper led a little group of people from the village out of Whispering Lane. She watched them coming. She recognized her mother's friend, Mrs. Dillon, in the lead. Then she heard a commotion coming from the cove.

"Throw down the anchor," said a voice from the beach below, breaking the silence around the coves and cliffs. A band of fishermen, led by Jimmy Hickey and Cod Nichols, were coming up the trail, dressed in kilts and eye patches and holding their swords in the air. Finished their work after a night at sea, setting pots and nets, it looked like there were ready to attack her. But no... they were coming to help her. She couldn't help herself and let out a loud whoop of joy, and to her surprise Jimmy Hickey whooped right back. And then she hollered again and he hollered and this went on until he was standing before her shaking her with one hand, holding a petrol can in the other.

"I love a good shout in the morning, clears the lungs and frightens the seals from the fish." He grinned a wicked grin and she could see his missing teeth and thick aging lines of his weather-beaten face.

"Me, too," said Chesca and the band of people gathered around her like her animals usually do.

Mrs. Dillon came right up to her and said, "I present to you, Miss Chesca, your troupe."

At first Chesca didn't know what to say. Then she looked at the faces of the grown men, all smiles and full of pride and Bamper beaming in his quiet way. He seemed delighted with his pirates and their costumes and kept pointing at them until she had to ask.

"What are you pointing at?"

"Watch," he said.

Jimmy Hickey took the petrol can, swigged from it and passed it around quickly and the six men dropped to their knees and struck a lighter to their mouths and blew a stream of fire. Chesca stood back and Mouse darted to the deepest corner of her pocket. The flames united in the middle of the circle and became one huge flame for a brief moment.

"Pure, crazy, magic," Chesca said, "You're the best pirates I've ever met."

And now all the men were up on their feet and wiping their chins and nodding at their own performance.

"Not just pirates," said Jimmy, "but musicians, singers, stage builders, lighting experts, men of acquiring great seating, men of great knowledge in all things," he laughed, a deep jovial laugh. "The best of men."

For the first time in a long time, Chesca smiled. "Thank you, thanks for coming. Ma would be so happy to see you, her dear friends."

Chapter 30

And so the rehearsals began and each night after everyone had gone home and the animals were exhausted from all the commotion, she curled up by the fire with her cloak and books and slept, comforted by the sound of the breeze in the trees and the waves lapping on the shore. Turkey watched over her from the oak tree. There were eyes everywhere on this mountain, watching silently. She had been sleeping under the stars since Da had signed away the farm. At first she thought Aunt Dena would go to Dublin Hospital and tell him, or come looking for her herself, but nobody came.

She picked up her list from the makeshift table under the tree. Mouse jumped out of her pocket and pitter-pattered over the log pile to a blade of meadow grass. A drop of dew splashed her face. She hummed a few bars of the song about Grace O'Malley.

Chesca tied her hair in a bun and stoked the embers of the fire with a branch. She knelt down and watched the first flame jump back to life.

"Has it been weeks already, Mouse?" she said.

"Weeks of madness," Mouse said.

"Oh, don't be such a Nelly," said Chesca, but Mouse was right. The rehearsals had been chaos with the crew by day and training with the animals by night. Jimmy Hickey had set his shirt on fire while practicing his newest trick. (He had jumped into Babbling Brook, no harm done.) Star had nearly pulled a tendon. The costumes were still being hemmed together by Maro and the arena looked a long way from magical, with wood strewn everywhere and wiring sticking out willy-nilly from the new stage. Cod took being a pirate to heart and when he was smoking on the hay bales then spitting flames he set fire to the electrical pole and Bamper shouted at Cod in a deep, frightening voice, as he put the flames out. As far as Chesca could ever remember, Bamper had never raised his voice until that day.

As they soldiered on, patient, the story of Grace and Malley was slowly unfolding, and she knew she was becoming a stronger trick rider and her confidence grew.

She placed another log on the fire. The sun was breaking through the clouds on the horizon. The mountain slept. Not a breath of Wind. It was the type of day when anything could happen: a day, a week, or a month that is roused with a whisper of great hope.

"Full rehearsal today," Chesca said and broke the solitude. She could hear the pirates coming up from the cove now. Jimmy Hickey began his morning holler.

"Do you want Star?" Polly said. She loved being the messenger girl.

"And the old ones," said Chesca. "Tell Comet their cloaks are ready."

Polly galloped off, splashing through Babbling Brook toward the lower meadows, where Star and the ponies were grazing.

Bamper and the Malone boys had come to finish building the stage. It was tucked into the circle, between the cottage and the trail to the cove. The old pews from the renovated church had appeared one morning, and Chesca had decided not to ask Jimmy how they got there.

Take a bow, Wind said, and blew around the cottage and stage, moving the red net curtains, and playing with her hair.

"It's a bit early," she said.

Little steps, sang Wind.

Chesca heard a diesel engine and Tom Malone, her father's friend, came bouncing over the moors in a massive red tractor. Mrs. Malone drove, leaning out the window, waving. He looked like a Viking with his red beard and arms like tree trunks. The tractor stopped near the cottage door and the Malones climbed down. Mrs. Malone opened a Thermos and poured cups of coffee for the gathering crew around the fire.

Mr. Malone tipped his hat. "Morning, all," he said, and walked among the men, joking with the pirates, clapping backs, shaking hands with the musicians. He was a good farmer and a great auctioneer. He could sell you calves or colts in a flash, and was renowned for his lively comments at the auction block.

"Thanks for coming Mr. M, I know you're busy with the calves," Chesca said.

Mr. Malone laughed.

"What exactly am I to be auctioning?" He looked at her, a little less jovial. "Cows? Are you selling the cows, Chesca O'Brien?"

"Not at all!" said Chesca, "the very thought of it, God no. Art, paintings of Howth, horses, waves, hills, boats, that kind of thing."

"Are they your paintings?" he said, studying her.

Chesca laughed. "I can't draw to save my life, but a friend of mine can paint very, very, well."

"I love art. Who's the artist?" said Mrs. M.

"Mr. Andrew Rooster," said Chesca, "he's not very well known." Chesca whistled, and Star walked over. Mrs. Malone looked at them, at the way they stepped precisely together and the horse leaned down a little for Chesca, as if she was asking her to jump up. Chesca threw her cloak to one side and swung her leg over Star's back. Mrs. M looked at her husband, and he raised his eyebrows.

"Small works or large?" he asked.

"Huge. They'd be great over a mantel or in a museum," said Chesca, running a hand over Star's coat. "All on canvas, framed with driftwood."

"Oil or water?"

"A kind of clay, oil and water mix, sealed with beeswax," she said.

Mr. Malone cocked his head to the side, pulled his cap off and scratched his forehead.

"Asking price?" he said.

"To be determined," she said.

"When can I see them?"

"Soon," said Chesca.

"Do we get to meet the artist?" said Mrs. M.

"He's very shy," Chesca said.

"I do like a quiet man," laughed Mrs. M. winking at Mr. Malone, who let out a raucous laugh.

The strum of a guitar began on the banks.

"Thanks, Mr. M.," Chesca said.

"Sure, can't you call me Tom?" he said. "Seeing as we're in business."

Chesca smiled. "All right, Mr. Malone, I'll call you Tom."

Jimmy pulled out the petrol can, put it to his mouth and tipped the can. He held the liquid in his cheeks then raised a flaming torch and with a burst, began blowing fire.

"Let's start from the top," Chesca said. She walked to the stage and looked out at the empty pews. The red curtain fluttered in the breeze, and Chesca took a bow.

Chapter 31

ut you simply must let me help, Frances-ca," said Aunt Dena.

Chesca stood in the hall and closed her eyes and thought of the million things she had to do. She had come to get clean jeans, her signs, and artwork from the loft, and cheese for Mouse. The show was less than a week away.

"I don't need your help," she said, taking a bowl from the kitchen cupboard.

"I'll design a poster for outside the church and the shop. You never know, you might get a few people to come."

Chesca had an idea.

"Aunt Dena, do you really want to help?" she said.

"Oh, I do. I think we got off on the wrong foot," she said.

Chesca decided her Aunt looked her most beautiful when she was telling lies.

"A poster for the village in your perfect script would be great."

"I'll get right to it," said Dena. "I want to meet the great people of this village."

"Wonderful," Chesca said, and stuck her chin out and held her head up. She could feel her aunt staring at her.

"Mr. Travers especially wants to help out," Dena said, walking from the room into the library and dining room. Chesca watched her every move.

Early sunbeams fell across the dark pine floorboards. Dust motes moved in the air. A smell of mildew hung around the clutter of boxes, folders, and shelves of books from the floor to the ceiling. Over the walnut table hung an ornate chandelier. Crystal drops tinkled in a soft breeze. The room was for dining and entertaining or simply reading by the fire with a glass of brandy in hand, but was neglected now.

On the table were jam jars filled with pens, crayons and paintbrushes. Dena pulled a large scroll from a bucket. She dusted off a chair, sneezed, and sat down to work, leaving the door ajar.

With Dena out of sight, Mouse came running from a hole in the wall and jumped onto Chesca's outstretched hand. Chesca put her in her pocket but held her finger to her lips.

Silence. She stood in the hall. There was a smell of cigar smoke, a blue tweed jacket on the coat rack and an oxblood leather briefcase beneath it. Chesca paused, listening, then knelt by the briefcase. Feigning a cough, she pulled the catch. It sprang open. There they were, the two sets of plans.

"Keep an eye out for the fox," she whispered to Mouse, and took out the blueprints.

"Don't," said Mouse. Chesca could feel her burrow deeper into her pocket.

"Mouse, for once will you be brave?"

"Frances-ca," called Aunt Dena.

Chesca peeked into the dining room through the crack of the door. Her aunt was sitting at the table.

"What's the name of the show?" Dena said, testing a pen to see if it had any ink.

"The Spirit of Grace," Chesca said.

"Grace who?" Dena said.

"You wouldn't know of her, Aunt Dena. She was a pirate from a long time ago."

"That old rabble rouser, I do know about her. Your mother liked her, but I would have had her hanged. She caused a lot of trouble, you know. I wouldn't say she'd bring you much luck, dear."

Chesca unrolled the blueprints. There were pages of diagrams and charts, and then she found what she was looking for: OLD BARN—CASINO & HOTEL. Under it was a duplicate copy.

There was a noise at the window of the front door. There was nobody there. It was just Wind.

Hurry, Wind whispered. Mouse trembled in Chesca's pocket.

"Gosh, it's windy out there," Aunt Dena, said. "She was nearly hanged, you know, that Grace one, but the dear old Queen spared her."

"Wasn't it the dear old Queen who wanted to hang her in the first place?" asked Chesca. She folded the duplicate and stuck it into her boot, pulled her jeans over it and closed the briefcase. The back door slammed. She kicked the briefcase under the coat rack.

"Looking for something?" said Mr. Travers. He was wearing his mucky wellies and wax jacket. He held a hunting gun under his arm and chewed on a cigar.

"I was looking for a mouse," she said.

"Yes, your Aunt mentioned that little problem," he said, and leaned the gun against the wall. "I think the traps should do the job." He walked into the kitchen.

"Tea, anyone?" he said.

Chesca sat down on the bottom stair. She heard him fill the kettle and place it on the stove.

"Yes, please," said Aunt Dena, moving into the kitchen.

Chesca willed her heart to be calm. "Be strong, be brave, be graceful," she whispered.

"Let's get out of here," said Mouse. "Let's show the prints to Da."

"What good would it do? He needs to see the truth for himself, Mouse. Anyway, I'm not afraid of them."

"I am," said Mouse, beginning to jump up and down.

"Do you think Grace would be afraid of those two? Mouse, we must win this on our terms, before it's too late."

"Wait for Malley," said Mouse, but Chesca was up off the stairs and striding into the kitchen.

"Talking of hanging," Chesca said, "Have you ever thought about it?"

Aunt Dena looked at her.

"Good Lord," said Mr. Travers. "What sort of a conversation is this?"

"Hanging and hell, they kind of go together, don't you think?"

"Is there a point to all this nonsense?" said Aunt Dena.

"Lying, cheating, greed." She looked out the window at a butterfly. Its wings beating, it floated with the breeze. Mr. Travers and Dena stared at her in utter silence. The clock tick-tocked.

"I would imagine," Chesca said, "if one was guilty of such crimes as these, they would be thinking about hanging and hell a lot." She kept her hands in her jeans pocket. Sometimes she was afraid of what she would do next, when she thought about the lies and deceit, sometimes she felt the red hot anger trying to burst out. These two were trying to kill everything she loved.

"One might," said Mr. Travers, "but they don't hang people nowadays."

"Don't they?" said Chesca. Malley would hang them off the cliff edge in a heartbeat.

"No," said Aunt Dena. "And lies aren't crimes."

Chesca turned from the window.

"Eight o'clock." she said.

"What?"

"Eight o'clock, the night of the show. I'll keep you special seats, right up front." She smiled. "And if I were you, Mr. Travers, I'd put that gun away. The last hunter to walk on this mountain spent three weeks next to a horse thief in Dublin Hospital."

"Loco," he said to Dena and twirled a finger around his temple.

Chesca threw him two fingers in the victory sign, and walked out the door.

Chapter 32

Let's see sparks fly," Mrs. Dillon sat in her director's chair with a megaphone to her mouth and her rose tinted glasses on the tip of her nose. Onstage the pirates were fighting with swords and axes from the props box of the drama society, roaring like madmen. A zip line had been run from the oak tree to a post on the stage. A rope hung from the line.

"Try that," Cod said. Cod was Jimmy's right hand man on the fishing boat and now in the show. Jimmy leapt off a barrel, caught the rope and swung through the air, landing on a bale of straw.

"Next time, no straw. We're pirates, not ballerinas," said Cod, lighting a cigarette.

The pirates slapped their thighs and laughed out loud.

Mrs. Dillon went for a cup of tea.

Cod took the end of the rope and climbed a ladder to the pirates' perch in the oak tree. He took a pull from the smoke and waved to his audience below.

"Jump," shouted Jimmy. The pirates began to clap and chant. "Come on, Cod."

Peter, the musician, began a tune on his whistle. Polly began to bark in time to the music, and Cod jumped.

He shouted as he flew, passing over the pews and crashing into the old oak barrels on the stage to great applause and whistles. He picked himself up, turning his head this way and that to make sure his neck wasn't broken. The rest of the pirates ran to climb the tree.

"Wait," said Maro, who was there for the day to make sure all the costumes she had made for them were fitted right. "You're going to fly over the crowd onto the barrels. Right?"

"Right," said Cod.

"Well, let's try that wearing your skirts, now, boys!" Chesca smiled and Maro hid her grin as the men put on their kilts.

At dusk the troupe gathered around the fire while Chesca rode around the circle, standing on Star's back. She extended her arms.

"Steady, Star," she said.

Maro watched her from her chair by the fire, as she stitched a hem. Beside her, Mrs. Dillon adjusted her glasses. The rest of the crew were folding their costumes and rubbing their aches and pains.

"I want you to know," said Jimmy, "that I saw the two of them, the aunt and the silver fox, at the restaurant the other night. Oh, they're going to build all right, but not a stud farm. No siree."

"We believe you, and we believe Chesca," said Mrs. Dillon.

There was a murmur of agreement.

"The truth will come out," said Mrs. Dillon.

"You know that Dena one has been spying on us, hiding behind the gorse bushes and watching. Does she think no one can see her?" Jimmy grinned. "Even I can with my one eye." He rubbed his eye patch. Everyone nodded. "It's Howth, we all know what's going on."

The fire crackled. Chesca slid off Star and joined them. "What will it take for Da to see the truth?" she said.

The sun was going down, leaving a red glow and yellow tint, the summer evening glow. People everywhere were taking in their hay, and going for ice cream floats after a hard day's baling. Nobody mentioned that the lower fields had yet to be cut.

"Your Da's not himself since your mother went to hospital," said Mrs. Dillon.

"I don't know who he is." Chesca looked at Turkey in the tree. There was silence. "And I hope my mother never finds out that her sister is trying to sell the land from under her."

"She thinks she's helping your mother," said Mrs. Dillon. "I dare say she's also trying for a husband with the

Travers man. People do funny things in difficult times, bless."

"I know," said Jimmy, always the one to see the bright side. "I mean, would you look at the state of us?"

They looked at Jimmy in his tartan skirt, hairy legs and eye patch. Bamper looked at Captain Covey, who was polishing his musket and Mrs. Dillon with her bullhorn, dressed in her pencil skirt and purple Wellington boots. She had a plastic bag tied tightly over her curlers to stop the summer dust getting into her hair.

"Now tell me we're not doing funny things in difficult times," Jimmy said, and laughed. Cod joined him. Turkey gobbled and they all laughed until the tears were rolling down their faces. Her mother and father had picked some real characters as friends.

There was the snap of a twig in the woods, and Malley stood in the shadows. He was rarely seen now around the cottage and circle. It was so busy at the Brandy Banks that the animals gathered in the lower meadows.

The elder horses, all twelve of them, had arranged themselves in a column, four abreast.

"Are you ready to show them, boys?" said Chesca.

Comet twitched his hairy upper lip and they moved forward and surrounded her, capturing her, capturing Grace. They tossed their heads and marched her out of the circle.

"I see we have our army," said Maro with a tight smile. The once strange behavior of Chesca and her animals now captivated them all.

Chapter 33

At midnight, long after the costumes had been neatly folded away and the cows and hens were sleeping in their beds, the Mountain fell quiet. Chesca and Mouse went to the hospital.

Her mother lay with the blanket drawn up to her chin. A full moon shone through the window. Chesca guessed by the way her Ma's silk scarf was tenderly tied—covering the stitches from her operation and her cropped hair—that her father had been here. A wild rose lay by her cheek. There was a peace to her. She nearly looked happy, unlike her father, Chesca thought, who had looked so withdrawn and troubled the last time she saw him. Well, he was troubled, it was the day he signed the farm away, the day he refused to believe her, the day he gave up hope. Before her mother had been taken to hospital he would never have sold the farm. But, she thought, he had lost the will to fight. She took a bottle of Maureen's peach milkshake from her backpack.

"The last batch before the show, Ma. The best batch."

She placed it on the bedside locker for Nurse Veronica to give to her. She leaned down and whispered.

"The older horses have never been so excited. Even Pig is optimistic." She brushed her Mother's forehead with a light kiss.

"Our little mountain looks magnificent, you have to see it, Ma, the show and the dancing are amazing, and Donkey is going to walk out at intermission with his basket of fruit. The kids will love it."

She adjusted her mother's scarf.

"Wish me luck."

Good luck, she imagined her mother saying.

From her backpack Chesca took a flyer for the show and left it on the bed under the rose. Quietly, she slipped out of the room.

In the corridor she heard someone coughing, and a radio playing classical music behind a closed door. She walked a little faster. Her green eyes looked grey in the cold empty corridor, as if the place drained the color and took the life out of a person.

She wanted to search out her Da, tell him to come home, tell him that everything would be all right. She wanted to see his broad smile. She wanted him to swing her in circles until she could not stand from dizziness.

But as she left the hospital, Wind met her.

Come home, Wind whispered.

"Da," she said, walking towards the car park.

No, Chesca, you must go forward.

In the star-filled night, in the quiet of the railway tracks, Wind gently guided her home, to where her friends were waiting.

Chesca slept under the stars one last time before the biggest night of her life. The moon lit up the Brandy Banks. It cast a silver sheen on the ocean. Malley stood asleep beside her and Polly lay curled into a ball. A breeze played in the treetops. Every night Chesca had thought about Grace, had felt her presence, but in her sleep tonight Chesca felt her mother. In her dreams, she saw her soft, kind face and her gentle hands. She felt the warmth of her mother with her.

She came in and out of a light sleep. The petals of the hawthorn tree nodded in the breeze; soon the wind would take them.

Chesca heard her.

You'll be great, said Ma.

"I wish you were here."

I am here.

"Malley is very calm. Has he lost his fight, like Da?" Chesca said.

He's a clever horse.

"I wish I were as brave as Grace."

You are brave. Look what you've done.

"What if no one comes? What if I fall off and people laugh at me? What if no one believes me?"

Listen to your heart, and to Wind. Ma smiled at her. *Courage is the true magic. It is what makes your dreams come alive.*

Chesca turned in her sleep, her vision of her mother getting dark and distant. She could make out feathers on the ground, loose downy feathers caught among the fiddlehead ferns and heather. Ma bent down and picked them up. A chill wind beat around the mountain, a mist made her face shine.

Beware of the fox, Chesca. He is hungry and he is close.

"I will catch the silver fox," said Chesca.

"No," said Mouse, springing up from under the cloak.

"Mouse, you must be brave, too," said Chesca. "You must be brave now. You must."

Mouse looked at Chesca. Chesca remained sleeping, her face peaceful.

"I will," Mouse said, on the verge of tears. As the last embers of the fire died, Mouse paced up and down and thought about all the ways she could be brave.

"I must face it," she squeaked. "I must."

Chapter 34

hesca met Mrs. Dillon in Whispering Lane early the next morning.

"Is Captain Covey ready?" Chesca said.

"He's down the pier now, readying the Asgard. It's like he's been waiting his whole life."

The path along Babbling Brook was lined with torches stuck in the ground, ready to be lit and show the way. Bamper had hung all of Chesca's seashell chimes from branches in the oak tree. Wind would make melodies. Even now, there was the softest tinkling. Mrs. Dillon pushed her glasses up the bridge of her nose and surveyed the work.

"How far we've come in just a few summer weeks," said Mrs. Dillon.

The show grounds looked like a Greek theater. Extra seating had been cut into the banks, in a semi-circle: a Greek theater, but Irish in color, with lush greens, purple heather and the yellow flower of the gorse. The front pews had been positioned with room beside the arena for the children to gather.

A gold curtain had been hung. Lights were strung along the front of the stage, down the aisles, and around the oak tree. Mrs. Dillon had planted petunias and geraniums in flower boxes and half barrels in front of the cottage.

A cream-white tent stood beside Babbling Brook; its high top billowed in the breeze. Bunches of white balloons were tied to a trellis in front of the tent. Chesca and Bamper had worked late into the night, setting up the inside. They had divided the tent into four sections, each with its table of wares for sale: hen's eggs painted silver and gold, with Rooster's sketches of Howth in black ink, Chesca's heart-shaped rocks and all the hand painted signs from the barn. Trick-riding lessons, taught by Chesca, were offered for sale and the milkshake stand took the centerpiece.

Chesca and Mrs. Dillon walked through the tent, straightening the tablecloths and tying balloons to the legs of tables.

"I hear there may be a few farmers coming tonight," said Mrs. Malone holding up a bottle of pink shake. "We've worked very hard getting this milkshake perfect. Watch out for them, they'll all want the secret to your cow's milk."

"Oh, they're just happy cows," Chesca said, moving on to the table set up for the Kerry Cows' milkshakes. She didn't really know if there was any secret.

A table covered with seafood and farm vegetables prepared by Senorita O'Rourke (a fisherman's new wife), ready for intermission, stood in the middle of the tent.

Everyone stopped what he or she was doing when Maureen the Kerry cow walked into the tent, to the cows' table, flicking her tail. She pushed Mick O'Rourke out of the way. Mrs. M looked as if she had something to say but could not. Maureen scrutinized the sign, "O'Brien's Marvelous Milkshakes." She sniffed at the cups beside the large tin vats of milkshakes.

"That's one pushy cow," said Mick O'Rourke. Everyone watched her to see what she would do next.

Maureen wandered out of the tent, looking back and giving Chesca a low moo that said she was happy, very happy. In a split second Chesca caught a glimpse of a purple wrapper, a Cadbury's milk chocolate bar wrapper, stuck to Maureen's hoof. There was another silver wrapper hanging from her tail. Someone was feeding them chocolate!

"Maureen, have the girls been eating chocolate?" Chesca said, and everyone looked at her. Chesca went a bright red being caught talking to, so directly to, a cow.

But Maureen was already walking away with a hip-swinging, tail flicking that said, ask no questions, tell no lies.

Chesca looked from the chocolate wrapper to the sky and laughed.

"BAMPER!" she cried.

Chapter 35

can be brave," Mouse murmured, standing in the tall grass, looking up through the blades.

Chesca was talking to Donkey, reminding him to get his basket filled with little bags of hazelnuts and pears for the kids. He was standing by the cottage in the sunlight, his white coat groomed. The shaggy hair around his ears had been trimmed and his black hooves polished. The show was less than an hour away.

Boots trudged around Mouse, barrels rolled by her and there was danger, a nervous excitement everywhere. She squeaked and ran after Chesca, dodging what looked like the heel of Mr. M's steel tipped boot. She popped her head over a buttercup, saw Chesca, jumped onto her shirttails and scampered into her pocket.

"I will be brave. I will be brave," Mouse whispered in the dark.

"I need my book, did anyone see it? *The Magical Horse Show.* It's my good luck book," Chesca said, searching through the pile of lists and books and pens.

The cast, the loud fire spitting, pirates dressed in full costume, all sat around the fire. The Cod fella jumped off the stone wall and tossed his feathered hat onto his head.

"Earl of Howth, heir to the castle." He practiced his one line repeatedly.

Mr. M pulled up on his tractor with sandwiches and bottles of Coca-Cola from the Monk's Tavern. He was singing, happy, as he had seen some of the artwork: Howth scenes of the the stallion in a full rear, of Julia the Spanish dancer who came to dance with Star in a fiery flamenco move, and Chesca riding Star, her eyes cast down in a pensive look. If buyers came, he said, it should be an easy night for him. He had made a few calls to art collectors he knew. Chesca was delighted.

But Mouse worried. What if they came and didn't like Rooster's art? What if they didn't come, what if...Mouse stopped. It was excitement that was brewing around her. Even the cows, as they settled down to watch the show, chewing, mooing, and pushing each other for better positions, looked excited.

Chesca worked with the horses. She rubbed a soothing ointment on the old one's legs, massaged the cool gel of mint and aloe into their splints and scarred fetlocks.

"Just keep taking deep breaths," Malley said, addressing everyone. "Keep your eye on Chesca and your ears to Wind."

Star took several deep breaths. Her gold cloak rippled across her back.

Malley walked out of the shade of the forest and stood in front of them. The sun shone through the trees. "Friends," he said. "Be proud. Your paintings are exceptional, Rooster." The old horses raised their heads and the cows stopped chewing. "Friends, it's time," he said. "You dance like a dream, Star, you are a shining star." She pawed the ground and the bells around her fetlocks jingled. "And Chesca, you once said you wanted to be chieftain of the East Mountain. Now, you are." Mouse loved how Malley spoke to Chesca. They were so strong. She could never be that strong.

Chesca looked at Malley, his eyes a steady calm not the wild fiery eyes of defense or the raging eyes for injustice. One day, he would really accept her as a chieftain. She wanted to tell him that a true leader would be allowed to ride her main horse, but now was not the time. Star would be upset.

"Good luck," Malley said.

Chesca returned to looking at the pile of books and notes and sketches she had by the fire. She scratched her head and looked to the trees. "I need the good-luck book."

Mouse remembered seeing it on the bedside table at the house but said nothing.

"Whatever happens," Malley said, "let's keep cool and don't let the silver-headed Travers and the aunt upset or distract you. Especially you, Chesca. Believe me, they will try."

Wind blew through the treetops, and the leaves of the oak sounded much like waves on the ocean. Outside the forest the first petals of the hawthorn fell. It was now or never for Mouse.

"I can get it," Mouse whispered. "I can be brave." She jumped out of the pocket.

"Come on, Polly," Mouse said. "Chesca needs us, she needs us to get the book."

Polly looked at Mouse who seemed to have gotten a little bigger.

"Right, let's go," Polly said and Mouse jumped onto her back and hung on to her collar. Polly galloped towards the house.

Chapter 36

olly stood under Chesca's bedroom window waiting for Mouse to throw the book down.

Mouse stood in the hole in the wall and surveyed the kitchen. She heard Dena coming into the kitchen by the click of her heels and she began to shake, but pushed herself on and popped her little fat head out of the hole to make a break for it, up the stairs and to the bedroom. Dena was getting ready to leave; she stood in front of the kitchen mirror and began talking to herself. Something about the things a woman must do, and something, something, to keep from being lonely.

Mouse could feel a slight tremble in her legs but she kept willing them to move forward. All she had to do was scoot past her and up the stairs, push herself and the book out the window to Polly and get back to the Brandy

Banks as fast as possible. It was getting close to show time.

"Scrape, scrape, pitter-patter, rattle-rattle of the window, all night long," Dena said to the mirror. "All night, the creatures, the trees, the wind. But pay no mind, Dena, you will prevail." She brushed her long hair. "Push on, push on. But..." she stopped, pointed at herself, "the rehearsal looks good, quite entertaining. Not exactly what I had pictured, who'd have thought..." She applied a coat of mascara to her long lashes. She placed a jeweled clip in her hair.

Mouse couldn't wait any longer, and did the bravest thing in her whole life. She put her toe out and kept it out, nothing happened. She couldn't see any traps or pellets or axes, so she made a dash for the kitchen door.

Polly sat panting with impatience. She kept her eyes to the window and began to get worried and started barking instructions to Mouse. "Hurry, hurry on, Mouse. Time to go. Chesca needs us. Push the book." But nothing happened and she sat back down and waited.

Mouse was like a bullet, flying across the room, her little paws hardly touching the floor.

"It'll all be over by Monday," Dena said. "Then me to the altar, beasts to the slaughterhouse…"

Mouse turned her head and looked up at the sound of the word, slaughter, the word that put the fear of God in Pig and the fillies and the cows. She didn't see ahead of her, only a flash of Dena's ring and the click of Dena's heels coming after her. She was still running when she hit the mousetrap set by the kitchen door. There was a snap and she heard herself squeal.

"Aha…finally," shouted Dena in her cold excitement. She picked Mouse up, lifted her by her tail trap and all, and held her dangling over the flames. Mouse squealed louder.

"Well now, could you be her friend?" Dena said. "The friend she talks to all day?" She looked a little closer. "You are, aren't you? You fat little rodent." She took the trap off Mouse's tail and dropped her into an empty jam jar and screwed the lid on tight.

237

She raised the jar to see her catch and tapped the glass.

Mouse looked out at Aunt Dena's highly plucked eyebrow and the last thing she felt was her head hitting the glass wall as she passed out.

Chapter 37

The people came. They came from every direction of the county and by every means possible. Tractors packed tightly with young lads from the Young Farmers of Ireland Association, the Dairymen of Munster, banners announcing the Dublin Horse Society breeders club, the Irish Pony Club, a group from the knit and bake club of Dublin, battered old cars driven by the Farmers for Organic Food, all coming in response to urgent invitations sent out by Mrs. Dillon. They were all friends of Mr. and Mrs. O'Brien, made over the years at horse shows, country fairs and plough competitions. Slowly they made their way up the hill through the village of Howth.

Malley and Chesca walked towards the cliff edge, took the bridle trail and stood above the cove where the Asgard lay waiting. The sun was setting into the ocean. Chesca wore her costume, her dress of beige, with her denim shirt over it to keep it clean. She looked back towards the cottage. She wondered how the old horses would do, if their legs would hold up with the marching. She thought about Pig standing on the corner of the main road wearing a sign with an arrow and hoped he would direct some people to the show. She thought about Malley, and how protective he was, and what a clever horse he was, and she worried about that shy but brilliant singer, Tighie Connell, being too nervous to sing, and God, don't let the pirates set anything on fire. She bent down to retie her bootlaces.

"Look," Malley said, tossing his head toward the main road. From the village to the turn for the farm the road was packed. Trucks, buses, horseboxes and cars inched up the hill.

"Malley!"

"Chesca?"

"There's a lot of people," she said. Malley kept his eye on the road. People crowded the footpath. The cars and people were moving at a snail's pace.

"Are they...coming here?" Chesca said.

"Or they're lost," said Malley, teasing her.

"They are," she laughed, "they're coming for the show. Look. They're turning for Whispering Lane." She hugged Malley's neck, and he swung her around in a circle.

"For once, Chesca—and now is the time—will you open your heart and mind to what it is that you really want? Challenge yourself. Give yourself the freedom to see that you do want those girls to respect you, to love you. It's what we all want, to be accepted. Believe it. Those girls are fascinated by you. They wish to be like you."

"Don't be silly, Malley. I respect you too much. Those girls don't like me because I'm different." She looked down to the wild grass, and the long stemmed ferns. "They call me crazy."

"Do they? Or is that what you imagined they called you? What was it that upset you, crying or Mary Murphy saying that everybody dies?"

Chesca thought back to the day Pig Senior died. It was so long ago and she was so upset he was gone.

"Everyone dies, Chesca. She is right,"

"But not Ma."

"Just not now," Malley said, "nobody is going to die now. We have a show to put on, Ches. You'll see," said Malley and gave her a nudge on her arm.

"Right Malley, nobody is going anywhere," Chesca said.

"Now let's give them a show to remember."

In the meadows the Malone boys hustled to guide the cars, trucks, and buses into the lower fields. The first patrons began the walk down Whispering Lane to the Brandy Banks. When Cod saw the crowds arrive he came running down the bank.

"There're coming by the hundreds," he shouted, and tripped in the ferns, tumbling head over feet.

"Get up Cod, we've no time for messing," said Mrs. Dillon, she shifted in her director's chair.

Cod sat up. "They're coming by the hundreds, I tell you," he yelled.

Mrs. Dillon whipped off her scarf and went to greet the first arrivals at the entrance to the tent.

"Calm," Chesca whispered. "Calm."

"Calm," said Malley.

But it was impossible, everyone was milling around getting ready. The butterflies in her stomach fluttered and danced. Dusk was setting in. She put a final coat of black polish on Star's hooves then looked out from behind the hay bales that hid the cottage and watched a steady stream of guests chatting and laughing, coming out of Whispering Lane and walking along the brook. The torch flames danced, casting light on each face. They looked at the wild flowers and heard the tinkle of the chimes as Wind played with them. There were families, lovers, the Boys and Girls Scout units, a group from the old folk's home being helped on walkers. Chesca recognized some girls from school and felt her fists tighten, then remembered Malley's words and let them relax a little.

But something was not right. She looked over at Malley, who was standing with the old horses now. She ran through the checklist in her mind: her cloak, Star's bells, tighten Donkey's basket. Julia was practicing her dance, her multi-layered skirts flying in circles. The pirates were all kilted and ready around the fire. But something was amiss. Something did not feel right.

The animals lined up in the woods. The hens took their positions in the trees, the cows by the hedge. Cod Nickels blew a huge flame into the night sky. Jimmy Hickey adjusted his kilt and eye-patch.

"What time is it?" he said. The cast had gathered behind the hay bales looking out over the circle and the benches.

"Ten to eight," said Maro, straightening costumes, then she threw Star's new gold cloak, the cloak for the show, over her back and buckled it at her chest. Malley stood beside the gate like a statue. The animals stared at the stage.

There was the drone of the tractor, generating the power for the cottage and lights. It belched a puff of smoke every now and again.

"Counting down," Chesca said.

"Head high," Malley said.

The elder Malone boys began seating people. On the bank Peter and Joe O'Neill began a soft tune on the fiddle and whistle. A tall, well-groomed man with pearl-white teeth moved along the front pews looking at the arena and the stage.

"Anne, can you believe this place? It looks like it's straight out of a fairy tale. God, I love this country."

His voice wasn't loud but had a force that carried.

"We have people from overseas," Chesca said.

"Loads of them, kiddo," said Jimmy Hickey. "He's my new friend that I met in the pub last night. He's an American, goes by Jay Jones and it looks like he kept his word and brought a busload of tourists."

They began taking pictures and filling up the pews, reading their play bill and gazing out to the lighthouse and Wicklow Mountains as they took their places.

"Five," Bamper held up his fingers and tapped his watch.

The seats were filling up fast. The guests held milkshakes in paper cups and the bidding paddles that came with the playbills. Chesca recognized Pablo, her tennis coach, still in his white shirt and shorts. And there was Nurse Veronica talking to—she stretched to see—a big woman in a beautiful orange dress. Her schoolteacher was here, and the principal, and even the school bus driver.

But the seat Chesca had reserved for her father was empty.

The tree rustled, but Wind said nothing.

Then she saw Aunt Dena and Mr. Travers. The tallest of the Malone boys escorted them to their seats. As she had promised, they sat up front in the shiny church pew. Mr. Travers did not look happy. Aunt Dena looked beautiful, radiant and relaxed, keeping her hand inside her wrap and chit-chatting with people beside them. Mr. Travers shook hands with Dr. Nugent and Judge Hilliard.

"What is she lying about now, Mouse?" Chesca said.

Cod tapped her on the shoulder.

"Standing room only."

Chesca nodded as words failed her now.

He pointed at the banks. The lights were down and the music stopped. The Howth Boys Band began to drum. Star began to fidget, snorting and stepping in place, jingling the bells on her fetlock.

"Let's go," Chesca placed her hand over her chest. "Mouse?" she said. She remembered leaving her shirt on a bale of hay and tried to remember when she saw her last.

"Go, darling," said Mrs. Dillon, waving her onto the stage.

*Ladies and Gentlemen...*Bamper began.

"Mouse?"

Go, whispered Wind.

Bamper was finishing the opening narration. She looked at Malley: he nodded toward the stage.

"Where's Mouse?" she said to him.

Don't think, just go, said Wind.

"I can't do it without Mouse," she said. There was a loud breakout of barking and she could see Polly rushing towards them.

"Mouse went to the house to get the good luck book," she said, "and never came out again."

Chapter 38

The curtain rose and the people clapped, cheered, whistled. Chesca stood frozen on the stage. The audience stopped applauding and an uncomfortable silence hung in the air.

"Grace," Bamper said. But Chesca still did not move.

Aunt Dena looked like she was in heaven; she patted Mr. Travers on the knee.

A warm wind came from the Mountaintop. Ladies brushed their hair back into place, and men gripped their caps.

Little steps to greatness, Wind said.

She looked at Malley, he stood gazing out to sea and she followed his gaze.

Wind seemed to diminish and a gentle girl's voice came to her. "It's time to shine," said the voice. Then

Chesca saw what Malley saw, a vision in the mist—Grace among the whitecaps, riding a white horse. The horses and the waves were one, and she moved with them. Chesca felt the cloak warm her, and hug her, and the gems sparkled.

"All your friends are here, even the smallest one," came the voice of the girl in the mist.

Mouse was here. Aunt Dena had her.

A farmer coughed and a baby began to cry. Chesca took a deep breath. Wind blew gently on her face, drying away the tears.

Bamper picked up the story. *Grace O'Malley was born...*

Every eye was on Chesca as she walked into the circle. The audience began to clap, except for the two in the front row. Chesca looked at her aunt, making sure to catch her eye, and raised her hand.

Star galloped into the arena, prancing and snorting, her gold cloak shimmering. The show began.

Chesca did not see her father, and those who did, hardly recognized him. His face was covered in a beard and he had lost weight. He sat on the grass on the bank, unaware that his name was on an empty seat in the front row.

Chesca flipped and stunned the crowd for a moment. She could see Mary Murphy, Aileen and Maggie Smith and a few other faces from school blurred in the light. She recognized their faces but could not read them. They sat with their mouths open and didn't move. Malley was just being kind; they were here to ridicule her. She did one more back flip while moving on to the next scene.

The story was moving quickly now.

But her father wouldn't let her go to Spain...

Chesca grabbed a rope and swung through the air, landing beside the barrels. The music stopped and Joe O'Neill picked up the bodhran. Chesca took the blade from her boot. She gathered her hair in her fist and looked towards the ocean, then to the audience. As the drum beat she cut into her thick locks, slicing until the hair came away and her head was downy as a fledgling's. Her hair fell to the floor.

She heard someone shout her name; it sounded like her father, but his seat was still empty. She held her hands up and begged the question: was she, Grace O'Malley, not as good as any boy? Was she not capable of going to sea? Was she not acceptable to her elders? Was she not accepted because she was different?

The audience, shocked at first, began applauding. Chesca ran toward the wing, cartwheeled and disappeared offstage.

And she stowed away on the last ship, sailing out of Clew Bay and into history as Ireland's Pirate Queen.

The audience let out a cheer. There was a shout: "Go on, Grace." Chesca recognized a young fishermen shouting from the rise of the bank. Yes, the fishermen would love Grace; she rode the waves for a living, like them. There was a huge burst of flames as the pirates run onto the stage. They blew flames over and over. The people in the front rows shielded their eyes as Cod set a torch to the pile of wood and a bonfire jumped to life.

Let me warm your spirits, for it is said that on the night of the harvest celebration, love is in the air.

Backstage, Chesca hurried to get ready for the next scene.

"Your mother would be very proud of you," said Maro.

"It's nothing," Chesca said.

Maro untied the dress. She pinned a wig of long tresses onto Chesca's head and slipped on her white shirt, then helped her buckle her chaps. Chesca, dressed now as Grace-the-young-woman, climbed the straw bales and watched the audience.

Love is in the air, Bamper said.

A young boy grinned at a girl across the aisle from him. He winked; she blushed and turned away with a smile. Love was in the air, but Mr. Travers did not look very loving. He was getting more uncomfortable by the moment, constantly looking over his shoulder at Judy Pennywise from the planning office. The woman could turn the whole mountain into a Casino with the stroke of her pen but right now, she looked to be enjoying the show. Aunt Dena sat perfectly still. Chesca watched for any sign of Mouse.

One at a time, the pirates climbed the oak tree and came flying over the audience's heads on ropes, landing on the stage. Chesca followed them up, took a rope from the line and swung, soaring through the air, lightly landing on the stage. She back flipped three times, pulled out her sword and began fencing with Jimmy Hickey. More applause. The wind was still, but the waves pounded the rocks with each clash of sword striking sword. Jimmy Hickey did his roar. His one eye looked ready to pop out. The children huddled in front of the pews leaned away from him and screamed in delight.

Then came the chatter of castanets and the beat of flamenco music as Julia twirled and Star danced. By the time the old horses marched into the arena to the beat of the drums, the audience were on the edge of their seats. They booed and jeered when Bamper told them how Grace was finally captured and taken to jail.

The old horses marched Chesca out of the arena, a wave of glistening manes and stamping fetlocks, and the audience murmured, wondering how she commanded the twelve horses without a word or without any tack, just their red cloaks and a drum roll.

The lights dimmed.

"Intermission everyone, and please, put your hands together for the Senorita," said Mr. M.

With the spotlight illuminating them, the Malone boys, now dressed in white shirts, came out of the tent with trays of the Senorita's food. They began serving the people in the front pews, working their way back. The people were chatting and laughing.

Mrs. Dillon held back the gold drapes and Donkey trotted out in front of the arena. He brayed and stood beside the children, and they jumped up and took little bags of nuts, pears or apples from his basket, petting him and pulling his ears. He was in Heaven.

Polly had sniffed out Da; she trotted through the crowds until she saw him sitting on the bank.

"She cut her hair," he said, rocking slowly and running his hand over his eyes. "Her beautiful hair." Slowly he raised his head. "What have I done, Claire?"

he said, as if she were sitting beside him. People were talking noisily about the milkshakes, the music, and the costumes.

A man with a newspaper sign, the Irish Harp, on his lapel sat beside him and kept scribbling notes. Not a banker: a newspaperman, a man good for the show, maybe. Polly eased closer.

"You're some man," Da said. "Pure blind, can't see the truth if it hit you on the head with a bat."

The newspaperman looked at him.

"Would you look at her, putting on a production, a production nothing short of Broadway, all to try and save the farm."

"I heard the child was taking on the big boys," the newspaperman said. "Boys who want to build a casino."

"A casino?" said Da.

Polly was going to bark at him and try and drag him to Chesca and let her explain everything he needed to know because he remained clueless.

"I'd say she could do it too," said the paper man, licking the end of his pencil. "I'm hoping she does. Makes for a good story."

Da looked towards where Dena sat, but with the intermission lights and torches all anyone could see were the faces of friends, Mrs. Dillon, Cod Nichols and Jimmy Hickey. Polly watched him nod to farmers he'd known since he was a boy. Slowly, like a thaw, Chesca's dad began to look a little brighter and he began to stand on his feet.

Chapter 39

Mr. M carried a podium to the center of the stage and tapped his microphone. He pulled his gavel out of his back pocket. Chesca, Jimmy and Cod lay on the stacked hay and watched the audience.

"Tonight, up for auction," Mr. M said, in his rapid auctioneer's voice, "we have the first of a series of exquisite paintings by Mr. Andrew Rooster."

There was a cackle in the oak tree that made people look up, but in the darkness no one could see the tiny eyes looking back at them.

"A local artist, so he is," Mr. M said, and put his notes to one side. "The first painting is of Chesca O'Brien. Well, I should say Grace O'Malley, looking out over the waves with her golden horse. Simply stellar, who will start the bidding? Can we hear a hundred?"

The Malone boys came out into the circle with the first of Rooster's paintings. It was a large canvas, a portrait of Chesca and Malley at sunset. The painting had been sealed in a glossy coat of beeswax and sun baked dry.

The crowd was commenting now, discussing the painting.

Chesca put her hands together in prayer.

"Rest easy," said Jimmy, and patted her shoulder.

"A hundred big ones to begin," said Mr. M. You won't get the like of this anywhere else, for your mantel or your foyer. Who will start the bidding?"

The tall man with the American accent, Jay Jones, stood up. He raised his paddle in the air.

"I'll bid one hundred," he boomed.

The audience cheered.

"We have a bidder," said Mr. M. A big smile shone through his red beard.

From the other side of the benches a woman in a halter neck dress and cashmere wrap, her brown hair pulled back in a turquoise clip, raised her paddle. Bamper directed the spotlight on her.

"Do we have two hundred? Is it two from Ruby O'Neill, art collector for the elite, and a fine eye she has," said Mr. M, pointing his gavel at her.

"We do!" she said, using her playbill as a fan.

The American bowed to her in a gentlemanly fashion and smiled, showing his perfect white teeth, then raised his paddle.

"We're on," Mr. M shouted, "we are in the game, will anyone join us? We have a bid of three hundred. Will it be just the two—and might I say what a handsome pair they are—will it just be the two of them bidding tonight?"

Mrs. Dillon, being the biggest matchmaker in Howth, did a little jump of delight, as she recognized a match when she saw one. Ruby, the art collector, raised her paddle with a flirtatious smile. The American countered her bid. They glanced at each other as they continued bidding.

"Eight hundred pounds! Unbelievable! You saw it here first: Andrew Rooster setting a record tonight." Mr. M pointed the gavel at the American. "Do we hear nine hundred?"

Chesca held her breath.

"Why the heck not," he laughed. "I haven't enjoyed myself this much since high school."

At the back a large older gentleman, with a pipe dangling from his mouth and a large gold ring on his finger, stood up. He looked hesitant, but his wife gently pushed his elbow and his paddle went up in the air.

"A thousand pounds! There is new blood on the block here, ladies and gentlemen. We have a new bidder. Are we going for eleven hundred?"

Mr. M looked to the American. He shook his head, and the audience let out a disappointed cry. Mr. M turned to Ruby O'Neill and she waved her playbill. No.

Then she beckoned to a little boy to come to her and she wrote a note while he waited. The boy ran with it to Mr. M.

"No others bidding?" Mr. M implored, and shook his head. "Sold! Sold to the man with the pipe," he shouted and slammed his gavel on the podium. He covered the microphone with his hand and read the note. He looked over at Mrs. Dillon who stood by the curtains.

"Ask Chesca how many pieces she has in total."

Mrs. Dillon made her way across the stage to the hay bales and looked at the cast, searching for Chesca.

"Next up," Mr. M said. The Malone boys carried out a painting of the mountain by moonlight.

"Chesca," she said, catching her breath, "tell me, do you have many of these beautiful paintings?"

"I picked my favorite five, but we have hundreds," she said.

"Darling, did you say hundreds?"

"Hundreds," said Chesca.

Mrs. Dillon pushed a bale of hay out of her way and made her way back to Mr. M and whispered in his ear.

"Ladies and gentlemen, we are pulling the artwork," he shouted. The audience booed.

"Why's he stopping?" Chesca said.

"Mr. M knows what he's doing," said Jimmy.

"Can the people who are serious about the paintings come and see me in the tent?" he said, and banged the gavel closing the auction. The beautiful woman who went by the name Ruby O' Neill, followed him. The American watched her, then excused himself and walked to the tent. Chesca could tell that Mrs. Dillon, sensing the power of love at first sight, quickly followed with a little twinkle in her eye. Her match-making skills might be needed.

In the shadow of the oak tree, Chesca fixed Star's cloak for the hangman scene. She glanced at Aunt Dena. The fire lit her face as she applied her lipstick. She put her hands back inside the Pashmina. Mr. Travers shifted uneasily in his seat, his foot tapping his brief case.

Back to what it's all about, ladies and gentlemen: Grace and Malley, Bamper said. The audience cheered and Chesca jumped onto Star's back.

Chapter 40

Word had spread across the banks and through the pews that Thomas O'Brien was in the crowd, but Chesca was galloping full speed into the arena. In the circle she pranced in a dance of negotiation with Julia the dancer, dressed as Queen Elizabeth. They danced a slow dance but Star tried to out-dance her, throwing her fetlocks high in the air and exaggerating each step. Chesca and Star cantered in a tight circle, around the ballerina and queenly-dancing Julia, the circle getting smaller and smaller until Star pivoted on only a hind hoof. Julia, in her red Queen-Elizabeth-like wig, was the picture of composure. Chesca wore her cloak and her long chestnut tresses looked wild and beautiful. As they met, looking at each other, breathing hard, the Queen bowed her head and saluted Grace.

And the queen, who admired Grace for her courage and determination, granted Grace her freedom, Bamper said.

The audience applauded and the drums beat out.

Aunt Dena and Mr. Travers looked very uncomfortable now and he made a move to get up but she put her hand on his arm and guided him back into his seat.

There was more applause as the curtain rose and people recognized the backdrop of Howth Castle. Mr. Travers shook his head, sour faced and squinting his eyes.

But the Earl refused Grace...

The crowd gasped as Chesca galloped in a circle standing on Star's back. The crowd were on their feet clapping. As she exited the arena, one arm raised high, she looked up to the sky and heard cheering, and knew they were winning. She caught the eyes of Mary and Aileen, standing side by side, to her utter surprise, wildly cheering her on. A cold chill crept alone her spine. Could Malley be right?

Polly followed Da. He was making his way towards Dena and Travers. He worked his way past the children in front of the pews, but then turned suddenly and walked toward the cottage.

Meanwhile, Chesca as Grace O'Malley was furious. Ted, Julia's six year old son, had the small part of the Earl's grandson and Chesca scooped down and put all her energy into picking him up. Like a sack of potatoes she laid him across Star's back. She galloped out of the arena to another cheer. Even Dr. Nugent's wife, a woman known for her coolness, smiled, snapped her fan shut and applauded.

The explosion of a musket made everyone jump.

"Look! The tall ships!" A lanky kid stood up and pointed to the cove.

Everyone turned to see what the kid was talking about and began surging forward to see the ships.

Bamper quickened the pace. *The Earl of Howth set sail after Grace, with a ransom; ready to fight the notorious warrior for his grandson's release.* He directed the floodlight on the Asgard as she set sail, and the three tall ships surprised even Chesca, moving swiftly around the lighthouse point, towards the cove.

Wind began to blow, and the Asgard moved out to sea. *The three ships set off, chasing her; chasing Grace.* The audience was quiet.

Chesca, backstage, said to Maro. "Where did those ships come from?" She slipped into her gold dress; her most beautiful dress.

"Captain Covey, it seems," said Maro, straightening the hem of the dress, "has friends in high places. They left the Tall Ships Race in Cork two days ago to be here tonight. For you, Chesca." For the second time in five minutes, Chesca let the idea, the very thought, that she really did have someone out there that cared about her, someone that was not her parents or Bamper or Malley and her farm friends. It began to seep into her thoughts and nearly distracted her.

The audience were on their feet, cheering. Chesca took one last peek to see if her father had arrived. His seat remained empty.

Malley stood at the edge of the woods, watching, as the curtain went up. Cod as the Earl, in a ruffled shirt and tights, wearing gold rings and a gold medallion and chain, stood in front of Clew Bay Castle. He held out a bag and a handful of gold coins. Grace spoke to the Earl.

"I have only one request: that your gates remain open and a place set at your table for a traveler in need."

Cod, earl-like, nodded and walked over to the fire.

"I have a gift for your boy," Chesca said.

The drummers began. A piercing whinny cut through the night. Wind blew the fire, sending smoke across the circle. As it cleared, Malley made his entrance. He galloped so fast he took the audience by surprise and rose on his hind legs and struck the air with his hooves. Chesca stood by the fire. People could see the whites of Malley's eyes and some wondered if Chesca should approach him at all. He whinnied again and pawed the ground. He galloped in a circle; divots of grass flew in the air and the children ducked. He halted in front of Chesca. Ted and Cod were walking out of the arena. Malley was supposed to follow them, but he did not.

"It's time," he said.

He tossed his mane and forelock and pawed the ground. He moved one fetlock forward and lowered himself 'til his forelock touched the ground.

"It's time," he said again.

"Malley."

"Do you hear me?" he said. "The time is right."

Chesca looked at the audience. All was quiet. She picked up the ends of her golden dress and with the other hand gripped the long strands of his mane. The girls in the front row watched her, not moving, every eye in the audience was on her. Wind blew gently, blowing strands of hair from her face.

Chapter 41

olly saw everything. She saw Chesca take hold of Malley's mane and she saw Da push open the door of the cottage, and she followed Da because he was about to learn the truth. She wanted to be able to tell Chesca all about it. Even if it were too late for him to do a thing, he would now know that Chesca had been right all along.

"Thomas. It's yourself!" said Bamper. "Would you look at this." He put the microphone to one side and opened the playbill to the last page. "Take a look," he said, Thomas looked at the playbill but it was Chesca that caught their attention.

She was running a hand over Malley's neck, and she spoke to him softly.

"For the love of all that's holy," said Da. "Tell me she's not going to ride him?"

"She knows what she's doing. Look at the playbill, Thomas," Bamper said.

Polly stood at the cottage door panting while Da looked at it. The last page folded out into a map, a copy of plans for the conversion of the barn into a casino, the house into a hotel, and a pool where the orchards were. Under it was a letter of objection, with hundreds of signatures.

"Where did you get these plans?" he asked.

"Chesca got them," said Bamper. "Stole them off that Mr. Travers. The stud farm Thomas, all a lie. Judy Pennywise from the planning office told me, fair play to her."

"Am I the last to know?"

"Chesca tried..."

But Da was already out the door. It slammed behind him and he nearly tripped over Polly and went slap-bang into Judge Hilliard.

Little steps, Little One, sang Wind. Chesca sprang onto Malley's back and held his mane, and she thought she would never let go. Malley was pulling himself up. Wind blew, and the flames illuminated Chesca's face, her rosy cheeks and the curve of her smile. Wind played the chimes and all the elements of the Mountain sang a sweet song, Brook babbled as loud as he could, and below them the waves lapped a merry tune.

Joe O'Neill picked up the flute and began to play, making nature's music a little sweeter. Joe looked at Peter. Peter shrugged. They had not rehearsed for this.

The music sent a shiver through the crowd; it was so delicate and spirited. They let it wash over them, all the time watching the horse and Chesca. Many of them knew of Malley and had heard the stories of his wild ways.

"Mouse," whispered Chesca in Malley's ear.

Malley sprang forward, and Chesca felt as though she were being thrown at the sky, flying. Never had she ridden a horse so strong. She sat upright and pulled the sword from her boot. Malley cantered around the circle and halted in the center. He stared at Dena. For the first time, they looked each other in the eye. Dena knew this was the horse they talked about. This was the wild one. She stood up. Mouse was trying to see past the folds of her Pashmina, but Dena held the jar under the wrap.

Mr. Travers was on his feet, starting to excuse himself. Dena broke from Malley's stare and looked up at the girl. Chesca tightened the grip on her sword and pointed it in the air.

"I believe you have my friend," she said.

Dena cursed and squinted her eyes at her. She drew the jar from under her shawl and held it in the air, her hostage. Malley and Chesca did not move, did not take their eyes off her. The audience, thinking this was part of the show, started clapping to the rhythm of a drum.

Dena started to follow Mr. Travers but Malley took a step. She stopped. She looked around her, and her gaze fell on the fire.

"Let me pass," she said to Chesca.

Malley was already moving, charging, and Dena raised her arm to throw the jar at the fire.

Chesca would never forget what happened next. The villagers would talk about it for years. Malley turned from Dena and sprang toward the fire, and as Dena threw the jar he jumped over the flames, sailed through them, while Chesca raised her right hand and caught the jar like a tennis ball and held it against her chest.

The audience were on their feet clapping. Pablo was waving his arms in the air at her and people were cheering, shouting her name again and again. Chesca looked at Mouse, alive but frozen in terror. Dena pushed her way through the children, knocking them out of her way. There was a loud squawking from the oak tree. Travers was heading towards the farm, back to his car.

Fog rolled in from below the cliffs and everyone became quiet. The tractor hummed, the lights still twinkled. Malley stood as the fog rolled in low and passed by them, ghostlike, and continued down towards the brook after Dena, to Whispering Lane.

"We have to get the contract, the briefcase," Chesca said.

And so it was, Grace lived out her days training young horses for battle, and as protectors of this beautiful land. Bamper was summing up the show.

Tighie was waiting for the signal to sing the closing song.

"He's getting away," Turkey gobbled, flapping his wings.

Malley reared and looked for Travers.

275

But now Da shook hands with Judge Hilliard and was walking out into the arena.

"Dad!" Chesca shouted. "Thank God, you came, they're getting away. Dad, Dad...the sons of..."

"It's all right child, everything's all right." Dad smiled at her, reached up and took her face in his hands as the tears fell and he watched the fear leave her eyes.

"Daddy, but...they have the contract."

"It means nothing, Chesca. I have something better." He pulled the microphone out of his back pocket and spoke to the huge audience.

He held up the playbill. "Look to the end," he said.

People in the audience began to leaf through their playbills.

"Over a thousand signatures," he pointed at the names. "Signed by you, and other people across the country that couldn't be here tonight."

Judy Pennywise, the director of the planning office, in a beautiful orange dress that had been gifted to her by Mr. Travers for all her hard work on getting the plans through, was sitting in the third pew back. She looked at the signatures in her playbill.

"Miss Pennywise," Judge Hilliard said. "Are there enough names here to protect the mountain? Forever?"

Everyone turned to her. There was a long silence as she studied her playbill.

"Do you have the originals?" she said, with the expression of a bulldog, for she was not too happy to be in the spotlight.

"I do," Mrs. Dillon said, loud enough to be heard on the banks.

"Well in that case," she said, "there are more than enough." And she did an unusual thing: she smiled meekly.

Another cheer rang out in the night, playbills were thrown in the air, and couples hugged each other. Cod Nickels ran with a playbill to show Chesca the names. He knew she didn't want to get down off Malley.

Her father stood beside her. "We'll sign with the planning board to make sure the mountain is safe," he said. "It will never be built on, ever."

Hot plump tears ran down Chesca's face. She felt his strong arms reach up as she sat on Malley and he hugged her. She smelled his scent of sweet hay and the smell of hard work that was ingrained in his clothes. He held on to her and whispered in her ear. "You've done a fine job...mighty." She pulled away, laughing and crying. He shook his head.

"And here's me, thinking you had a wild imagination. Well, it's powerful stuff, and I'll never doubt you again. You are, your mother's daughter."

Tighie began to sing an ode to Grace. In the quiet people began to sway and hum.

Grace O'Malley is sailing strong,

Grace O Malley is coming home.

The lights dimmed, except for a spotlight over the water, and everyone could see the Asgard sailing back toward them. The fog was gone. Da reached up and put his hand in hers. The hawthorn tree released its petals, and they floated, with help from Wind, over the cottage and audience, and fell like snow over Chesca, Malley, Da, and Mouse.

Chapter 42

Polly followed close behind Dena, sure she would cause more trouble. Polly had a nose for trouble since the day Dena had kicked her. When she entered Whispering Lane, spiders from the farm and neighboring barns huddled in the grass together, their beady eyes looking left and right. Above Dena in the leafy tree branches, hundreds of ravens and sparrows and singing birds, sat as still as possible.

Dena hurried after Devlin Travers who was just ahead of her now, walking at a brisk pace. He kept his hand on his hat as if a gust of wind might take it. He kept close to the trees. In the light of the torches, he looked wary and afraid. He sneaked. Polly thought he looked like a fox that had been caught in the coop.

"Devlin," Dena called, but he did not turn back. Wind blew, and the treetops rustled and the branches swayed towards her.

"Devlin, what about the penthouse?" she said, catching up with him. "We still have the contract."

He turned, as if hearing her for the first time.

Something moved in the trees.

Dena looked up, she pulled her Pashmina around her. A flame from the torch behind them went out in a puff of smoke and Whispering Lane got darker. Polly crept closer, trying not to pant.

"Penthouse?" he said, and pulled the playbill out of his jacket pocket. "Dena, dear, it's over. There are enough signatures here to stop a man from building a sandcastle."

Dena glanced at the signatures.

"The girl was busy, Dena, and has more friends than we could have ever imagined. In fact, Dena, I have a feeling she may be the one with a Plan B."

"What about us?" Dena asked. She remembered his words of endearment, *Dena, my lovely, sweet woman, beautiful touch, kind lady...*he hadn't meant them?

"Us," he said. "Dena, dear, the crowd may be looking for trouble in light of the plans. We should move. Do you think it wise to go our own ways?"

Dena hesitated. She thought she could love him. Something moved in the hedge. She shivered. The wind was picking up. There was a flap of wings from the treetop, something brushed off her arm, but Polly couldn't see what.

"Can't we find another project then?" she said.

"I think our project days are over. I invested my shirt in this one. I think I'd like to retire and take up...ballroom dancing."

"What?"

"Yes, it's a secret passion of mine, and tonight...well, tonight showed me it's never too late to begin."

"Well then...best of luck in your new pursuit." Dena said. "Ballroom dancing? I would never have guessed. I'm more of a ballet woman, myself."

They began the walk out of Whispering Lane. The treetops went quiet and Wind was calm again. The birds sighed and the spiders began to creep back home to their webs.

"May I walk you to your car?" Devlin asked. The gate flew open, but Mr. Travers merely glanced at it.

"Thank you, Devlin, how kind," she said.

The fog came tumbling down Whispering Lane and escorted them out. Polly began barking; go on, take off. Go back to Dublin. Don't come back...bark, bark, bark. But they took no notice of her, either.

They walked toward the house and their cars as Wind rose again in a breezy chuckle—a chuckle that grew to a laugh that continued for some days.

Chapter 43

Da was standing on a ladder, banging a nail into a large piece of wood above new pine doors. The Forever Farm was carved into the board, the lettering painted in silver. He banged the nail one last time and climbed down to meet his guests.

Rays of light shot through the holes in the roof, and the warmth of the sun gave the barn a tranquil, lazy feel. There was a low coo from the loft as Owl nested. Chesca wondered what in heaven's name Malley's story would be for autumn. It would be hard to top summer's story.

Dressed in her jeans and a new tee shirt that read *The Spirit of Grace* across the front and a graphic of a horse in a rear under it, Chesca crossed the breezeway and hung a silver sign on the office door: *Shows and Sales*. Then she hung a gold star on Star's door. She heard a woman talking to her dad and walked out into the sunlight. Jay Jones and Ruby O'Neill walked toward her and shook her hand. A man with a black peaked hat and suit stood by a large shiny Bentley.

"Nice to finally meet you, Chesca," Jay said, "I hear you'll continue with your show."

"All going well," she smiled.

"I hear you have some admirers that want to train with you?"

Chesca felt a blush rise in her cheeks. She had heard this too. She had heard that all the girls from the other stables wanted to be part of the next show, that Mary Murphy had bought all the trick riding lessons, but she had not seen them, they had not come to the barn or called or wrote, or even trotted past the gate.

Ruby went back to chatting with her dad about art. He was telling her how much Ma loved art. Ruby O'Neill had bought the whole Rooster collection and handed Da a check. The American and the art collector left for a walk around the cliffs and Da just stood there looking at the little piece of paper with the line of zeros that meant everything was grand.

"Don't you need to get to the bank before it closes?" Chesca nodded to the check.

"One cup of tea and I'll head down to see the baldie ol' ba…"

"One cup," Chesca said.

The phone rang. Chesca ran to the hall and answered it. At first she couldn't make out what the woman was saying. Then she nearly dropped the phone.

"Oh Chesca, dear, oh, this is good. Is your father there? Wait 'til I tell you."

"Nurse Vee?"

"Oh, Chesca, what was in that milk?"

Da was beside her now.

"Have I got news for you." She sniffed then laughed. "Your Ma is sitting up, says she's thirsty for a milkshake. I've never seen the like."

Her father hollered a whoop of joy and ran to the door, grabbing his cap and jacket and the front page of the newspaper that was hung on the wall. Chesca raced after him. He stopped, picked her up and swung her in a circle until they were both dizzy. Chesca released a cry of pure happiness, a cry she never knew she had. When they steadied themselves, her father spoke first.

"Look. You stay here," he said and took her by the shoulders. "A lot has changed. Let me tell her what happened."

"I'm coming."

"Sweetheart," he wrapped an arm around her. "You need to be here, you know, to welcome her home. Things have really changed."

Chesca knew he was right. She nodded and he kissed her on the forehead and ran out to the Jeep. He drove out past the gate with a honk of the horn. She could hear the horn blow again and again as he drove down the rocky road to the village, towards the city and the hospital.

She stood in the quiet of the hall and listened to the tick-tock of the clock. Wind came and rattled the window, and a draft blew through the house. The dining room door fell ajar with a creak, inviting her in, and she could not refuse. Dust motes danced in the light of the midday sun, and the old room, with its chandelier and walnut dining table and silk-covered chairs, still looked fit for a queen, a chieftain, and she knew what to do.

"Mouse," she cried, "Find the candles."

Mouse somersaulted out of her pocket and scurried to the cabinet.

Chesca blew the dust off the table and wiped down the china set and placed eight stemmed glasses on the sideboard. Under the table she found the tarnished and forgotten silverware box. She polished eight knives and forks until they gleamed. She laid a golden silk tablecloth with embroidered rosebuds, her mother's favorite. Finally, she went to the garden and picked a bunch of wild climbing roses, wrapped them in white ribbon, and put them in a vase on the table.

She made three calls: to Mrs. Dillon, to the Senorita and to Jimmy Hickey. A feast would be prepared, a celebration, friends would gather. She opened the heavy stiff windows and let Wind in. Wind played with the crystal droplets of the chandelier, which swayed and tinkled. Mouse jumped up on her shoulder.

"Hold tight," she said to Mouse.

Yessss, rustled Wind, as she ran toward the barn.

"What's the story?" asked Malley, as she burst into the barn and stood in the doorway under the new sign.

She jumped up and down. "One of your biggest fans is coming home," Chesca said.

There was an outburst of braying, screeching, and flapping inside the barn. At just the wrong time, Maggie Smith and Mary Murphy came trotting up the road and into the yard.

"Ma's coming home," she shouted at them. "Ma's coming home, my Ma!" Then it crossed her mind they would think she was totally crazy now. The animals were still going wild with joy, but they did the craziest thing, they jumped down off their fat ponies and gathered around her and jumped with joy too, and Chesca let them; she let them in.

Chapter 44

uiet now," Chesca said. Ma was due at any minute. The girls wanted to stay until she arrived and they stood at the back of the barn, watching, delighted to be part of the homecoming. The animals were standing at the huge double doors of the barn peering through the slightly open door, listening for the Jeep. She sat on Malley, her King. Her cloak around her shoulders falling down and across his back. She felt him shift slightly to look around the barn, then back to the gate.

The hens continued clucking and scratching and Malley gave them a cross look that quieted them down. The barn was silent.

The Jeep came into sight and the gate swung, as if on a spring, and landed with a gentle ping on the stone wall. Mary Murphy looked at Maggie. Donkey began to bray and Pig grunted.

"Steady, boys," said Chesca.

Chesca could see her mother sitting in the passenger seat beside her dad. She looked relaxed and happy, with her hand hanging out the window. Every eye in the barn was on her as Da drove into the yard.

"Now," said Chesca.

Malley pushed the doors open with his nose and trotted out. The younger horses began prancing and bucking. Star trotted on Chesca's left and Donkey on her right. Mouse sat confidently on her shoulder.

Da jumped out of the Jeep. He opened the passenger door and began to pick Ma up.

"I can manage, Thomas," she said, taking her first step back on the farm.

Da grabbed a red quilt from the seat and wrapped it around her. She walked a few steps with Da beside her. Everyone circled around her. Rooster flew onto Donkey's back, Turkey hopped up onto the roof of the Jeep. Polly went for the comfort of Ma's hand, seeking a pat. She had to lean on Da's arm. She held her breath, putting her hand to her heart when Chesca rode up to her, sitting on Malley like she had been born for this noble horse and he for her. They were a union of balance and grace.

Chesca gave a theatrical bow.

"Ches. Sweet, sweet Chesca. You look like a queen." Ma said.

"Chieftain!" corrected Da. "Chieftain of the East Mountain."

Da pulled a newspaper from his back pocket. Ma took it and held it up, pointing at a picture of Chesca and Malley on the front page of Arts and Culture.

"Chieftain," Ma said, and held out her arms to her daughter.

Chesca wanted to stand up and back flip off Malley, but she couldn't wait another moment; she jumped down and ran right into Ma's arms.

Not a bird moved or a pig twitched.

"Everything is going to be just fine," Ma said.

"Everything is," Chesca saw her mother acknowledge the girls with a kind nod. Da pretended to scratch his eyebrows and wiped away a tear.

Lightly, Wind circled them. Chesca looked toward the mountaintop, waiting for Wind to speak. Claire followed her gaze, and it was she who whispered.

"I can feel the mountain breathe." They held their gaze until Da kissed Ma on the cheek.

"Hey. Sleeping beauty," Da said, "Tell her about the cloak."

"It fits you well," Ma said.

"Was it yours, Ma? Did you make it?"

"I only re-stitched it, Chesca. The stitching was falling apart after all these years."

"But where did it come from?"

"I wanted to tell you the full story of Grace," she said. "Of how she sent the gift of a cloak and sword to the O'Briens after she heard that the stallion had come to this farm. Legend has it, she sent a messenger with these gifts and said that if the stallion remains free, he would protect us, and protect the mountain."

She looked at Malley, standing quietly beside Chesca, his dark eyes staring back at her.

"Grace wore this cloak?" Chesca said.

"That's what they say," her father said.

Chesca ran her fingers over the soft heavy velvet. She glanced back to the girls standing by the barn doors. They were red faced, teary and smiling. They were comfortable sitting bareback on their ponies.

Her mother hugged her tightly and whispered.

"Ches, you had the courage to see your dream become reality. You know, one day I'll thank my sister."

The trees swayed, and everyone looked skyward and listened to the gentle laughter of the wind and then for the first time, Chesca heard her girlfriends calling her, excited and impatient, asking her to start training, today—now.

Her Ma released her and she ran to join them.

Wind blew softly...*Chesca...I will be with you always...*

Chesca stopped suddenly. A cold chill rippled along her back. "What do you mean?" she whispered.

"Wind?"

Nothing moved, not a bird or a breeze. She looked back at her Ma and Da. They stood watching her, Da's strong arm across Ma's shoulder.

"Come on, Chesca, hurry up," Mary said. Her pony, Buster, began to chew his bit and paw the ground.

"I'm coming," Chesca said, but remained looking to the sky. She remembered the day that Pig Senior died. Wind came down from the Mountain and held her in a warm embrace?

"Wind, you're not leaving me, do you hear me?" she whispered. "Please tell me you're not. Can you hear me?"

Mouse was quiet in her pocket and even Pig was silent. Polly followed her gaze to the white clouds in the sky. Chesca closed her eyes.

"Wind?" she whispered. "Please don't leave."

A strong gust came into the farm and shook the trees and blew straw across the yard.

I said...with you always, now go on...hurrrrry. Wind began a soft chuckle. Chesca threw her hands in the air and let out a holler of joy.

"Ah Wind, you had me going there for a minute. Let's go have some fun," she laughed, shaking her head as her old friend Wind gently blew the hair from her face. Malley trotted alongside her and in mid-stride, Chesca jumped on his back and together they all rode down Whispering Lane.

Epilogue

1542 Clew Bay

 steady northeast wind blew, whistling through cracks in the thick stonewalls of the O'Malley castle on the shores of Clew Bay. In the great hall the chieftain clan sat among friends and elders at a long oak table by the fire. Some played a game of cards and listened to the musicians as they plucked harps and played whistles on a small stage. Others ate mutton and drank red wine from pewter mugs, discussing the upcoming voyage. The gathering was a farewell feast, before the clansmen sailed across the Atlantic Ocean to trade on foreign shores.

A twelve-year-old girl sat opposite her father, the chieftain Dubhdara. She held her cards closely to her, and then she told him:

"I'm sailing with you."

Grace O'Malley spoke in a low tone, so the elders would not hear her. Her chestnut hair fell forward like a veil as she leaned across the table. Her brother Donal shook his head and mocked her with a smirk. He too held his cards close to his chest. She ignored him. There was a crackle and spitting in the fire as a servant turned a boar over the flames.

"In Spain, you'll need me," Grace said. She did not falter or blink. Dubhdara O'Malley, took a long drink of wine and he did not look away from his hand of cards.

Look at me, she willed him. She knew she could win, that she would sail with him to Spain, if he would just look at her, but he remained focused on his hand, and he did not look pleased.

She glanced quickly down the table to where the elder chieftains sat. They laughed and talked among themselves. She knew they mocked her father for allowing her, his only daughter, to become such an accomplished sailor. On the contrary, it was her father who had taught her so well, but now he was resistant to taking her on board. She was making her pipe-playing brother look weak.

Dubhdara drew the king of hearts.

"Grace," he said, placing the card on the pile, "it's time for you to learn the skills of a woman and a future chieftain."

Her mother Margaret placed a card on his king with a smile that said she might have won the game.

"It'll be a dangerous trip and we don't need any long-locks on board—bad luck," he said. When her father spoke everyone paid attention.

"I beat you to Scotland last trip," she said.

The elders were laughing at her now, or was it him they laughed at? A flash of anger crossed his face. Grace bit her lip, closed her eyes and silently counted to three; she would have to be more careful.

She had grown up on these shores and knew every rock and rip tide around the inlets and trading routes of the west coast of Ireland. Now, she was eager to explore new waters.

Her father still did not look at her and she felt she was losing this battle, but she would not give up easily.

"You know I can get a better price for the mead than him," she said, tipping her head toward her brother.

The elder chieftains stared at her father, waiting, curious to hear his answer. The musicians picked up the tempo, banging drums and wildly playing fiddles.

"You," he said, "will stay at home. It's time to learn from your mother."

"Aye, good luck to poor Mother," Donal said, throwing a queen of spades onto the pile.

A young servant held her laughter, her face a glowing pink. She poured another tankard of ale. Grace held her head high, and swore at Donal. Then she threw down the ace of spades to win the game. Donal was furious.

"Go sharpen your needles, little sister. There are socks to mend," he shouted, pushing his chair back and kicking the hound.

"When there's a sword at your scrawny neck and your blood runs cold, you'll be crying out for my blade, not needles," she taunted him.

Her father looked at her sternly. "Grace," he said, "you'll make a great chieftain's wife, if..."—he held his finger to his lips—"you can curb your tongue."

"Wife?" she said, feeling the blood rise to her cheeks. "No, father, captain. Someone needs to fight and maintain the O'Malley territory."

"You'll stay home and learn the ways of a woman, Grace." Dubhdara dismissed her with a wave.

A stout red-faced watchman hurried into the hall.

"The winds are changing," he said. The chieftain stood and pushed his chair in.

"It's time," he said. Drinking the last of his wine, he bent and kissed Margaret on the forehead.

The music played on as the men began to gather their satchels, cards, and knives.

Grace hurried to her room. She pulled back the gold velvet curtains and looked out the tower window to a starry, moonlit night. The waves lapped gently on the rocks below. A seal popped his head out of the water and bobbed in the bay.

Her bedroom walls were covered with murals depicting battles on the lush green hills of County Mayo. The O'Malley horses were easily recognizable by their gold color and lead position on the field. A leather-bound book, The Aeneid, in Latin, lay on her bedside table. A fire crackled and flickered on the hearth.

Below, her father, brother, and fifteen clansmen, maybe more, pushed open the huge oak doors to cries of farewell and good wishes. Carrying torches, they walked briskly out of the castle along the moonlit bridle path to the shore and the quays and the waiting galleys. A pack of dogs barked at their heels. Grace could see the flames of the torches lining the quays in the distance.

"Darning holes for hairy toes is not my game," she said aloud. She buttoned her shirt and pulled on a pair of leather breeches. She laced her boots to her knees, pulled them tight and placed a short silver sword in the lining of each boot. She took her green heavy cloak and wrapped it around her. Instantly it warmed her.

All was quiet around the castle now. The servants would be busy in the kitchen, cleaning up after the rowdy farewell. Her mother would remain at the table with her guests, listening to the traveling musicians and playing cards with the carrow—the gamblers. The smell of smoked boar lingered in the castle and the night air, even *after it was packed in salt and carried to the boats with the oak barrels of ale.*

Grace whistled into the summer night, a sharp call, like the cry of a curlew forewarning a bitter winter. A herd of red deer startled on the hillside and moved into the forests. She whistled again. A golden stallion came galloping out of the woods and came onto the bridle path past the well. He came to a halt under her window.

Grace tested a rope tied to a hook in the wall. It was secure. She lowered herself backwards, out the old tower window. Her chestnut locks swung behind her as she sprang down the tower wall. Landing lightly beside the horse, she ran her hand over his neck. He stood calmly when she jumped on his back.

"Capaill alainn, my beautiful warrior, never fear standing tall, love will always conquer all," she sang softly to him. Besides from her mother and father, she loved this horse more than anything: this horse and the land he roamed. If ever she became a chieftain, she would ensure this horse was immortalized, she would keep his strong bloodline going, for generations to come. Ireland needed him.

She had trained him well and he listened for a command. She looked back to make sure no one in the castle had seen her. Inside a man shouted, the music continued, laughter erupted, but the castle gates were closed and nothing moved outside. A gentle wind blew and the horse began to prance.

"Go on."

He sprang into a canter, taking Grace into the woods and to the trail that lead to the quays. He galloped and snorted in the cool night air, leaving dust plumes in his wake. He came to a halt at the end of the forest, hidden in the shadows at the bottom of the oak-clad mountain. The quays lay only a stone's throw away. The darkness of the trees concealed Grace as she watched for her opportunity.

On the dock, hundreds of men worked quickly to set sail. A steady wind was blowing and she knew they would be casting off soon. The sailors pulled ropes, tested oars and rolled the last of the supplies on board. Caged pigs squealed and hens squawked as men pulled and stacked them. The scrape of metal on stone rang out as the men sharpened swords and tested axes. The blacksmith leaned on the bellows, sparking the fire pit.

He dunked a bayonet into a bucket of water, surrounding himself in steam and a violent hiss.

Some of the younger deckhands arrived from the village, late and drunk. Grace knew her father would punish them. Every hand was busy preparing for a journey that could last weeks or even months. Climbing down from the mast, young Brendan Kelly sang a song about his lost love.

The first rope was being cast off. Grace could hear her father shouting commands. It was time. She slid from the horse and took one of the swords from her boot. It shone in the moonlight. She held her locks to one side as close to the scalp as possible and sliced, letting the chestnut tresses fall around her feet. Again she cut, until her hair was cropped and sticking out in stubble. She blew loose hair off the blade and stuck the sword back into her boot.

She ran a hand over the horse's neck then took off her cloak. The jeweled garment would surely give her away as the chieftain's daughter.

"Now, do I look worthy of the sea?" she asked the horse. He kept his eyes on the dock.

"I'll give them holes in their socks, all right," she said, tying the cloak around the horse's neck and laying it across his back. Then she picked up the cuttings from the forest floor and tucked them into the cloak pocket. "Stand at the gates in the morning. When Mother sees you, she'll know I've gone to sea."

The last of the crew were in the ships, beginning to untie the remaining lines.

"Go on, brave soldier," she said, and he turned and galloped back into the forest. She crept along the forest edge until the first ship was pulling away. The second ship cast off. She sprinted and hid behind an empty barrel on the dock until the oarsmen pushed the last boat away. All eyes were on the waves of the Atlantic Ocean as Grace O'Malley leaped from the quay onto the stern and picked up a rope. Quietly joining the crew, she began to pull the sail into the wind.

"Trim the mast," came the command.

Grace sank all her weight onto her heels and heaved on the line, hard, as skilled as anyone around her. In front of her Brendan Kelly turned and looked at her. His eyes widened. She shook her head to silence him. He turned around and continued to haul on the line. He *would be loyal to her and he would be the first of many to remain a loyal follower. For as the fleet left the inlet of Clew Bay, she sailed into history as Grace O'Malley, the Pirate Queen, and there are some who believe, that she is sailing still.*

THE END

ACKNOWLEDGEMENTS

I would like to thank my family. My parents, Tina and John O'Brien who gave us kids the freedom to discover the magic of a little mountain and the love to make it a safe place. To my sisters and brothers who continue to support me without saying a word. To my friends who have remained friends even when the years and miles separated us, including Ireland herself. I love you all.

To my children, you know who you are. To my husband, without his encouragement, kindness and most of all his belief in me, I would never have put pen to paper and discovered the joys and challenges of writing.

To Helen Seymour, the best writing partner and friend you could ever want.

To my sweet Martha's Vineyard girls, and my DC sisters, I love and thank you. Lorin you have been a great listener on our walking, talking, trips around West Chop, thanks a million for all your support.

To the Indian Hill writing class that loyally helped me craft this work, Sue, Alice, Gary, Melissa and Anne and all the students of both classes, for your advice, patience, nit-picking, sharp observations and gentle understanding.

When it was time to release the work, author Anne Lister and Frank Sledd of SleighFarm Publishing have been tremendous and truly supportive of a new author.

To editor, Emma Dryden, of drydenbks llc, it was fantastic to work with a professional in the world of children's books.

To artist Chris Beatrice. Chris, did I tell you how much I love the cover?

To first readers, Ciara Seccombe, The Eddy girls, Mr Ruairi Mullin, Keith Chatinover, Jason Flood, Sue Hruby, Gerry Storrow, Sharon Ratcliffe and to one amazing children's book critic, Camille Cuzzupoli. Thanks to all my test readers who gave great feedback.

To Nancy Aronie for giving me a tiny glimmer, a vision, that writing is a beautiful art and for providing the safe place to begin, in the Chilmark Writer's Workshop.

To Gerry Storrow and Frank Sledd for line editing, any mistakes thereafter are solely my own.

When the student is ready the teacher appears - Buddah.

Finally, to my teacher, John Hough Jr, a wonderful editor and author, for practicing patience and kindness and sharing his steadfast love of the written word. For shining the light along the writing journey and for having faith in me, even when my fighting Irish spirit was at its best. Like any great teacher, you always have kind words at the right time. Thank you.

ABOUT THE AUTHOR

Lara O'Brien was born in Dublin and raised on the wild and wondrous hill of Howth, as in - Howth is Magic - a beautiful seaside town on the northeast coast of Ireland with cliff paths and moors of outstanding beauty.

She grew up one of many children who were part of Howth Riding Stables, a barn for twenty-five horses, cows and a clever dog named Polly. It was an adventurous and innocent childhood.

In the early 1990s the barn and land were sold with the promise of becoming a stud farm and was then quickly turned over to a developer. Planning permission was refused for 52 houses and since the economic downturn its future remains in the hands of a government agency.

She now lives on the sister island of Martha's Vineyard with her husband, four children and writing companion Tukka Rex, a great golden (and talking) dog.

Made in the USA
Charleston, SC
04 February 2014